Midtown Huckster

Leopold Borstinski

September 1931

1

THE NEW YORK Central building stood on Park Street between Forty-fifth and Forty-sixth. The place was built to be the heart of the city, resplendent with its marble lobby which stretched an entire block. Before nine in the morning on weekdays, you could guarantee the joint would fill with people hustling into and out of the thirty-five-story building.

On September 13, stood by the red elevator doors were four men in suits and long brown raincoats. One of them pressed the elevator button and they waited for the cab to return to the first floor. The tallest checked his watch while his nearest colleague commented under his breath, "Relax—we have plenty of time to get him. He won't be going anywhere for a while."

A nod and a sigh. Immanuel was right, but that didn't mean hanging around was any easier. If anyone had bothered to cast an eye over them, they would have seen the coats, the short haircuts and the black suits and shoes and thought they were looking at a bunch of government agents. Listening to their conversation, they would have assumed they were about to make an arrest.

The bell rang when the doors opened up and a herd of people belched out. The guys waited politely until the cab had emptied and they stepped inside. Immanuel asked for the ninth floor and the elevator operator acknowledged the request. When nobody else showed any interest in entering the car, the shutters slammed shut and the men stared at the ornate moldings and paintings of clouds on the ceiling.

◆ ◆ ◆

THE THIRD MEMBER of the group had a bulbous nose and pulled out a handkerchief as he appeared to cough and splutter his way during the upward journey. The rest of them ignored him, but the elevator man kept shifting his eyes toward the ill guy.

Two women got in on the third floor, chatting away to each other and ignoring the men standing in the same confined space.

"So do you think Hank's interested?"

"He asked you out for a drink and he seems very attentive around you. He doesn't give me the time of day."

"I don't even know if I like him that way."

"Have you seen the size of his expense account…?"

The elevator opened onto the sixth floor and the girls left before the men could find out whether Faye would be in Hank's clutches before the weekend.

Immanuel glanced at the other three as they all calculated how many seconds it would take from the time the door closed to the point when they'd be facing their foe. Almost as soon as they had blinked, the elevator bell pinged and the operator announced, "Ninth floor."

Immanuel, bulbous nose, and the other two stopped in the hallway to read the register of businesses and to figure out which corridor they should walk down. Eyes scanned the alphabetical list across all four columns until the *Castellammare Trading Company* popped out from the rest.

Next to the name was a three-digit number, 924 and to the left was a sign indicating that suites over 920 were along that corridor. Immanuel pointed in the correct direction and the guys checked themselves in a mirror hanging opposite the board.

Whenever an occasional person traipsed past them, the men turned round in a huddle to discuss some weighty matter and resumed their journey once the stranger had passed. Down the aisle and left through a set of double doors. Then they stopped outside suite 924. Immanuel looked at his compatriots.

"Are we good?"

"Let's do this thing," muttered bulbous-nose, as much to himself as to the group. Immanuel tapped on the door and the fellas entered the Castellammare Trading Company offices.

THE PLACE DIDN'T look like much—the anteroom comprised a desk, filing cabinet and secretary, along with two couches and two men sat there making the whole office look messy. They sprawled across the furniture as though they owned the joint, but a door to the right of the assistant showed there was another room where the leader of the enterprise resided.

"Hello, miss. Is the boss in?"

"Do you have an appointment, gentlemen?"

"I can't rightly say that we do, but we have an urgent matter to discuss."

The slouched men had sat up straighter as the conversation ensued. These flatfeet had appeared unannounced and the chances were that they didn't have a warrant.

Immanuel flashed a badge and explained that he needed to insist on getting to the inner sanctum.

"Sorry, but I am under strict instructions not to disturb Mr. Maranzano."

"So he is in, then?"

Claudia Valenti's eyes flitted to the guys on the couches and looked back at Immanuel. The fellas stood up, one facing the three guests and the other looking directly toward Immanuel.

"That is none of your business, mister. You need to listen to the lady and come back some other time. Make an appointment, why don't you?"

"As we are here, we might as well wait until Mr. Maranzano has a spare couple of minutes."

He nodded at the other three—bulbous-nose leaned against the office door and the other two squeezed past and sat on the couches, one on each. Maranzano's fellas shifted around the room to avoid having their backs to any of these agents. Immanuel sidled next to one of his guys on the couch who whispered to him, but he kept his eyes on the secretary all the while.

"I do hope we are not getting in your way."

"No, but I really have no idea how long you will have to wait."

"Why don't you start by letting Maranzano know we are here?"

Claudia sighed, knowing Immanuel was right but aware that she was about to get into trouble. She looked askance at Maranzano's men, who showed no interest in intervening.

She held down a button on her squawk box and spoke clearly into the microphone, "Mr. Maranzano, there are four gentlemen to see you without an appointment."

"Tell them to go to hell."

"They are from the police."

"What the..."

The voice trailed off and three seconds later, his office door opened and Salvatore Maranzano, mob boss appeared. He was annoyed that he had been disturbed, but despite his lofty position, he realized he should show the detectives at least a small amount of respect if he were to rid himself of these annoying insects. He eyed the four men and shrugged.

"I guess you'd better come in, then."

These words were aimed at Immanuel, and bulbous nose followed him in. As they walked, Immanuel gave the other two a simple instruction: "Keep our friends here occupied and make sure they don't leave the premises."

Before he passed the threshold of Maranzano's office, Immanuel cast his glance over to the whisperer, who nodded but remained silent.

"I SUPPOSE YOU have a warrant, or is this one of your friendly shakedowns?"

"We wanted to have a conversation to alert you to a problem you will shortly face. Of course, if you make any donations to the Police Benevolence Fund, that's entirely up to you."

Maranzano tutted and sat down. He'd heard all the excuses in the world from a thousand cops who wanted a little extra in their pay packets at the end of the week. It wasn't the request which annoyed him; he just didn't like being disturbed before his second cup of coffee.

"Spare me the sob story and get to the point. I've better things to do with my time than listen to the likes of you."

"What you got against cops?"

"Nothing that fifty bucks or a bullet don't fix. It's Jews I can't stand and I reckon there are a couple in my office right now."

Immanuel turned to his companion and laughed.

"What you know, Alex, he doesn't like us."

Alex guffawed back and clung to the edge of Maranzano's desk to stop himself from falling over with mirth. Meanwhile, Immanuel had moved to the other side of the old Italian, chuckling as he did so.

"The truly funny thing is, *Mister* Maranzano, that we have come here to give you something, not to ask for anything at all."

"What? You've brought me a gift?"

"Nah, a message."

"And what has a Jew-boy like you got to say to a man like me?"

Alex Cohen took one step toward Maranzano, whipped out a knife from his pants pocket, bent down and plugged the blade in Maranzano's stomach. The Mustache Pete didn't know what was happening until he looked down and saw a river of red leaving his guts.

Immanuel launched himself at the guy, pulling out his own shiv and stabbed him two, three, four times.

"Charlie Lucky says you will die like a dog."

Alex sliced at Maranzano's torso. Blood gushed out of every wound and the body slumped to the floor. The head banged on the corner of the desk on its way down, but it didn't make a difference because the self-styled Boss of Bosses was unconscious.

Immanuel popped round the door to see how the men were doing. They were standing over two corpses, but the girl was nowhere to be seen.

"Where is the secretary?"

"Immanuel, we told her to go for a long walk and buy herself a large coffee. She'll be out for the rest of the day."

"Should have killed her anyway, Vito."

"Claudia won't squeal. I know where she lives and she knows I do. Even if the real cops come knocking, she'll suffer a terrible bout of amnesia."

"You'd better be right."

"It'll be fine, Alex."

Back in Maranzano's office, the corpse was surrounded by a red lake. To make a point to those who survived him, Alex took out a revolver with its silencer, placed the muzzle in Salvatore's mouth and squeezed off one slug. There would be no open casket for that cadaver.

The men left the Castellammare Trading Company and headed back along the corridor. Near the board listing the companies on the ninth floor, they checked themselves in the mirror before calling for the elevator. When the red doors parted, the four members of Murder Corporation got in and Alex requested the lobby. As they descended, he thought how pleased Charlie would be to know that the last of the old guard in the Italian mob was no more.

2

CHARLIE LUCKY AND Johnny Torrio had formed the syndicate two years before, along with the elite squad known as Murder Corporation. With Louis Buchalter and Albert Anastasia, Alex was responsible for the smooth running of the group that killed other gang members at the request of the bosses of the organized crime gangs that ran the Eastern Seaboard as well as far-flung places like Chicago and Detroit.

The three men had seats at the syndicate table and, for better or worse, they had muddled along without treading on each other's toes too much. Charlie Lucky was the joint head of the syndicate, but you would be forgiven for thinking it was his entire show. Johnny Torrio preferred to spend his time counting his money and focusing on his own operations.

If Murder Corporation had a headquarters, then it was situated in the Jewish enclave of Brownsville within the confines of Brooklyn, east of Manhattan. While it was Louis' home from home, Anastasia preferred somewhere a little more Italian and was more comfortable in East New York or midtown. Alex always enjoyed staying on the island and had a distrust of the bridge and tunnel club.

Albert called a meeting of the directors and Alex suggested Lindy's Restaurant for a coffee and slice of cheesecake. He'd had a soft spot for the venue ever since his time spent there with Arnold

Rothstein before his mentor's untimely demise. They sat in a booth at the back, feet away from Arnold's old table.

"So what are we doing here?"

"Alex, first I hoped we would start with some pleasantries and then cover our latest contract a little later."

Louis laughed and winked at his old-time friend, Albert. "Ever in a hurry, Alex. You should learn to take things easy."

"Sorry, but there's always another buck to make and as you know, I don't like to hang around."

Albert turned to Louis, "How's the family?"

"No complaints, thank you, Albert."

"And the kids?"

"I imagine they are doing just fine. I don't see them that much, what with work and so on."

The two men maintained broad grins throughout this exchange.

"And how's your mistress? Is she well and looking after you?"

"Albert, I would say so for sure. You might be right if you figured the reason I don't spend enough time with my children is because of the excessive hours I enjoy in Ruth's arms."

Chuckles from the two men and Alex felt a bit of him die inside.

"Come on, guys. Enough is enough. All the people we love, sleep with, or pay maintenance for are in great health. Who's on the kill list?"

As soon as the words left his lips, Alex realized he had overstepped the mark—no direct references to the work they did should ever be uttered within earshot of strangers or anybody who didn't need to hear.

"My apologies, gentlemen. I let my impatience get the better of me."

"That's all right, my boy. We forgive you and you are right— business before pleasure."

Albert cleared his throat and spoke in a more businesslike manner.

"First on the agenda is a message from our friend, who thanks you Alex for the recent conclusion to the matter of our older acquaintance."

Charlie Lucky had worked for Maranzano almost the entire time Alex had known him, although the tension between them only became intolerable after the syndicate was formed back in '29. At that point, the old Sicilian guard refused to acknowledge there were fresh ways to function in the modern century and that Italians and Jews could work together for mutual benefit. In contrast, Charlie was the first to see that the New York melting pot applied to the criminal underworld as much as anywhere else in the city. He seized the initiative, helped in no small part by Rothstein, and figured out a way for every gang boss to dip his beak in the trough without pecking out anyone else's eyes.

"I'm glad everyone was happy with the outcome. The primary targets of our operation were all met, although I want you to be aware that a young woman fled the coop."

"Should we be worried about her, Alex?"

"No, as I am assured she won't squeal, Albert."

"Are you relying on the word of Tommy Lucchese?"

"Yes…"

"As much as Tommy is a good fella to have with you when the going gets tough, his desire to trust a skirt has put him in deep water previously, Alex…"

"And it would be a shame for him to sink to the bottom of the Hudson over this dame."

"Exactly, Alex, especially as we'd be the ones who'd fry."

"I shall take care of this oversight."

"Thank you, Alex. Let's not forget that loose talk costs lives."

"We live together, we love together, but we die alone."

They tucked into their cheesecakes, oblivious to the fact they were holding this meeting in broad daylight in a busy diner. The difference here was that Alex's lieutenants, Ezra Kohut and Massimo Sciarra stood guard near the entrance to prevent any unwelcome visitors inside the premises while they were there.

"Now let's move on to item two…"

CLAUDIA LIVED IN an ordinary tenement in Bed-Stuy, just north of Brownsville. Her time as secretary with Maranzano meant she knew far too much for a woman her age, but what was certain to her was that if she breathed a word to anyone about the four men who entered that office then she would sleep with the fishes.

She considered leaving town but figured she'd be too easy to find. So instead she holed up in her apartment and waited for everything to come good. Her best hope was that they had let her go in the first place—why release her to only kill her later? That idea permeated her mind until the following day when there was a tap on the door.

Claudia froze for a second because she wasn't expecting any visitors and, again she thought, it must be safe. What hitman would knock politely when they could kick the door down and murder her in her sleep? She peeked through the spyglass and saw a besuited guy, who seemed a bit like one of the four from yesterday. She shrugged and undid the latch.

"Come in, why don't you."

Alex doffed his fedora and strolled across the threshold and, with no further invitation, sauntered into the living room, quickly followed by Claudia.

"Thank you for seeing me, Claudia. I'm sure you must be at a loose end now your boss has met an untimely demise, so I hear."

"You know who I am."

"Tommy sends his regards." Alex knew the Lucchese name would offer the girl some comfort and put her at her ease.

"I understand it's an imposition but do you think I could have a coffee?"

"What? Sure, yes…"

Claudia wandered off to the kitchenette and busied herself with beans and her percolator. Although she hadn't noticed, Alex stood at the far end of the kitchen leaning against the refrigerator. She swiveled round to get some milk and jumped when she saw how close he was to her.

Despite her concerns, she carried on and waited for the water to boil and then she let the coffee bubble away in the upper chamber of the percolator. Alex remained still for the entire time.

◆ ◆ ◆

A LIFETIME LATER, Claudia poured the steaming brown liquid into two cups and put them on a living room table next to her couch. Alex unbuttoned his jacket and sat down at one end, giving her more than enough space without feeling hemmed in. As a precaution she sat in her armchair instead, a few feet further away.

"Thank you, Claudia."

"You're welcome, but I doubt you have come all this way just for a cup of coffee."

"Correct. Recently you found yourself in a situation and I wanted to check my people didn't make you feel the least bit uncomfortable."

"Oh no, not at all. They were very nice about it—suggested I went out to get a drink before any trouble started."

"Good. I'm glad. Sometimes my boys can behave inappropriately and forget how they must be respectful around the fairer sex."

"There's nothing to worry about on that score, Mr. Cohen."

Alex stirred his coffee and stopped as soon as Claudia mentioned his name. Then he continued and took a sip before speaking again.

"You know who I am."

"I didn't recognize you, if that's what you were wondering. One of your guys used your name and I put two and two together."

"You're a bright girl, Claudia. Have you been back to the office at all?"

"I figured you told me to scram, so I did just that. Yesterday evening's paper told me all I needed to know."

"Did they say who did for Maranzano?"

"No, only that it was gang related."

"And what do you guess happened?"

"Mr. Cohen, Salvatore paid me to do what he asked, not to think."

"Call me Alex. How well did you know Salvatore?

Claudia blushed and her eyes cast down onto her lap—the rumors were true and that she was one of his many conquests.

"My apologies, it was wrong of me to ask you such an indelicate question. Can you forgive me?"

"Of course… Alex."

"Perhaps you'd be interested in carrying on a bedroom arrangement with me instead of Salvatore. You're a fine-looking woman, after all."

Claudia's eyes flicked from left to right. She couldn't believe what Alex was suggesting, but it would explain why the gentleman had come calling.

"Well, a girl has to earn a living..."

"Why not start our new relationship now? Hop into bed and I'll be with you in a minute—I need to freshen up first. I hope you don't mind."

"Not at all. It's pleasant having a man around who cares about such things."

She showed him the way to the bathroom and once she'd headed to the bedroom and undressed, Alex popped by the sink and waited a count of sixty. Then he flushed the toilet, put his hand in his inside jacket pocket and strode toward the bed.

Claudia lay under the blankets with her clothes strewn around the room. She smiled coquettishly at him and Alex returned her grin. He pulled out his pistol and shot her in the head. Then he stuffed a pillow over her face and squeezed the trigger again. He threw ten dollars on her bedside table and walked out into the fresh air.

3

A WEEK LATER, Alex sat opposite his good friend, Alfonse Capone, slurping spaghetti in a restaurant controlled by the man who ran Chicago.

"I'm surprised you came over to do this job yourself. Surely you have minions to carry out your every whim by now?"

"There is a network of associates—and you have known that for years—but any excuse to visit a pal."

"Too kind. I suppose you've been reading about my difficulties?"

"The papers are full of them. How d'you get into this mess?"

"Alex, the simple truth is that I listened to my accountant. He told me I should keep records of legitimate business dealings so I'd have something to explain my income. Turns out, he was wrong. The disparity was too great between what I bought and the money I officially brought in. The court case has only got another couple of weeks and then it'll all be over."

Alex grimaced because Alfonse was likely to face prison time and every law enforcement agent in the country had been working night and day to bring the man to his knees. To them, he represented the worst excesses of organized crime.

"Do you think you have a chance to get off?"

"Only if I am able to apply some leverage to a couple of the jurors. I have the brightest tax lawyers money can buy, but I'm guilty and everybody knows it."

They continued eating their pasta course, but by the time the last of the tomato sauce had been mopped up with the final piece of bread, neither of them wanted to talk about courts and jail.

"The reason I am here, Alfonse, is to explain about the contract. The target is your underboss, Grimaldi, and I want you to know this is strictly business for me. There is no personal malice involved whatsoever."

"I appreciate your concern. If he must go, then so be it. He has made a mistake and will pay for his misdeeds."

"I'm glad you understand the situation, Alfonse."

"Alex, the fact you have taken the time out of your day to talk to me on this matter speaks volumes. Besides, I agreed to the hit otherwise Murder Corporation wouldn't have been given the contract."

They smiled at each other because they both knew Alfonse was right. Any hit between gangs was approved by the syndicate members, and only then did anyone engage the services of Alex's group. A silence grew between them, but they were comfortable in each other's presence. There was nothing more to say. Grimaldi was a dead man walking and Alfonse would soon be incarcerated for who knew how long. That'd be down to the judge, but the chances were, he would not receive a slap on the wrist and a couple of months behind bars. And this might well be the last time the two men would get to see each other for quite a while—neither wanted to express it, but they knew it. You could detect it in their eyes.

PEPE GRIMALDI WOKE up in a blue funk—he should remember not to drink so much. He looked around to find he was in his apartment and the snoring next to him showed he was not alone. Pepe turned to face the broad and admired his taste in women. He eyed her naked body and wondered if he wanted to wake her for some more fun. Before he could reach a conclusion, there was a knock on the front door. Probably the boys come to pick him up. He checked his watch and discovered that he was running a few minutes late.

A grab of a towel and Pepe opened the front door and headed into the living room without looking back—an icy blast of air hit his chest and he didn't want to hang around welcoming his guys.

Alex stepped inside and followed Pepe until the fella halted and saw the stranger in his apartment.

"Anybody else here?" Alex snapped.

"Huh? A skirt in my bed, but no one else."

"Tell her to stay there and she won't have any trouble."

"She's asleep—she'll be no bother to anyone for a while."

"Make sure it stays that way. And you'd better put on some clothes—we're going for a ride."

"Where to?"

"Does it matter? Capone has issued an order."

Pepe shrugged and clung to his towel, which was lurching toward the ground. He shuffled off to the bedroom and threw on pants, shirt, and jacket—the first items he saw because he'd got a sense from Alex that the guy didn't want to be hanging around while he attempted sartorial decisions.

OUT IN THE hallway, Pepe made to walk down the stairs, but Alex pointed upwards.

"I thought you said we were going for a ride."

"Yep, but first I want us to have a private conversation and you have a guest in your apartment."

"Okay."

Pepe wasn't sure he believed the guy, but his argument made a certain level of sense. Besides, Capone ruled the roost and if that's what Alfonse wanted, that was what he got. Six long flights of stairs later and they ran out of steps—just a door leading to the roof. Alex sidled past Pepe and tried the handle. It was locked but a quick push with his shoulder and they stood outside, on top of the world.

Alex sauntered across the asphalt and stopped to lean against the balustrade at the far end of the building. Pepe dutifully followed in his wake until they were facing each other. Silence for a second and then Pepe decided enough with these antics.

"So what do you want to talk about?"

"How are things going with you, Pepe?"

"All right, I suppose. Why?"

"I hear things. People chat, you know how they do."

"Don't believe everything folks say."

"I check the facts before I reach a conclusion, which is why you and I are having this conversation."

"And what do you think you have found out?"

"Do you like a drink, Pepe?"

"As much as the next guy, I suppose."

"From all accounts, more than the next man. You like to party, wouldn't you say?"

"Yeah, but I'm not the only fella in Chicago to drink and have a bit of fun."

"No, you're not. That is true. Would you say you can hold your drink?"

"U-huh. Every now and again I get a bit wild, but most of the time, I handle myself just fine."

"In a speakeasy, having a coffee laced with gin."

"Or vodka. I prefer vodka if I can get hold of it."

"Me too, Pepe. That's something we have in common."

"Nice."

"And when you bring a lady friend home with you, like you did last night, do you always treat them with respect? Offer them a drink from your private collection? Show them a good time?"

"Why yes, what's the point of bringing a woman back to your place if you're not going to have a fine time?"

"Pepe, that's my point. I asked you if you always show the broads respect and you told me you did, but we both know that isn't true, don't we?"

For the first moment since their arrival on the roof, Pepe understood where the conversation was heading. He gritted his teeth and steeled himself, back straightened.

"Like I told you, don't believe everything people say."

"And let me remind you I check the facts. Pepe, your mistake wasn't to rough up Erika Pisani, but you raped the girlfriend of an underboss and left her alive."

By this point, Alex had circled Pepe several times during their conversation and as he spoke his last words, he ensured Pepe stood between him and the balustrade. Alex stepped forward in an instant and punched Pepe in the solar plexus. He crumpled immediately, giving Alex the opportunity to grab him by his collar and throw him off the roof. Pepe Grimaldi had left the building.

4

HOBOKEN WAS NOT Alex's idea of a great city, but he knew that the easiest way for him to maintain some contact with his sons was to visit them rather than expect their mother to bring them into Manhattan. When Sarah walked out on him, taking their five boys with her, Alex's men found her within two hours of their search. Thirty minutes later, he knocked on the door of the hotel suite where they were staying. Her ashen face spoke volumes as he stood there and demanded his children back, which she refused.

Alex considered dragging their sorry asses to what was once their home, but deep down he knew he wouldn't be able to look after them better than their mother. So instead, he let her go and asked that he still have access to the kids. Sarah's initial reaction was to refuse and that made Alex dig his heels in.

Rather than overtly threaten her as was his instinct, he held in his anger and waited. Her original response morphed over the following weeks into the realization that the boys needed a sturdy father figure in their lives and there wasn't any man much stronger than Alex.

Ever since, each week when Alex was in New York, he would take time on Saturday afternoons to head off to Hoboken and play with Moishe, David, Asher, Elijah and Arik—in the park when the weather was good and in a hotel suite hired for the purpose when times were cold, wet or both.

The youngest three knew him as the strange guy who'd appear in their lives now and again, but they didn't feel a close connection to him. Moishe would never forgive his father for letting Arik get kidnapped, although the boy couldn't help but be grateful to his papa for saving him from the bad men who stole him away.

ALEX PUSHED ARIK on the park swing while Asher and Elijah played make-believe in a playhouse at the top of a small ladder attached to a set of monkey bars. Moishe and David sat on the grass a few feet apart from the others, too old for such juvenile pursuits as climbing or messing about. They would soon be teenagers and it showed in their behavior if nothing else.

The little one was having a wild time as Alex pushed him higher and higher until Arik believed he was flying over the world. His father smiled at the simple pleasure the youngest of his men was experiencing. It seemed good to do good.

All was calm in Elysian Park and the male members of the Cohen family were only thirty feet away from the corner of Hudson and Tenth Streets. Every few minutes, Alex would look around to check on his charges, but there was no danger apart from hurt pride or a scuffed knee. The pleasant thing about this recreation area was that when Alex looked east, he saw Manhattan on the other side of the Hudson and that made him feel closer to home than he actually was.

He gave Arik a countdown for his return to earth and picked him up high above his head and helped him to land on both feet.

"First one to Moishe wins."

Alex slammed his foot down for his first step and ensured that Arik arrived at the two lads before himself. Neither David nor Moishe seemed pleased to greet the runners. Alex hopped over to a bag he'd brought along, took out a baseball and shouted over to Moishe: "Catch!"

Despite himself, the eldest leaped up to grab the ball, positioned himself so it landed in his cupped hands, and rolled on the floor to increase the drama of the moment. Alex pulled out a bat from the same bag and organized a mini tournament. When it was his turn to face the bowler, Alex made sure he didn't put too much swing on the baseball bat and, for a second, a memory flashed across his mind of the days before the war. The blood-smeared recollection over, he spent the rest of the day focused on squeezing every valuable minute out of his time with his sons.

5

SARAH ARRIVED LATE at the diner and blamed the housekeeper for her delay. Alex didn't care who was at fault, he just wanted to see his estranged wife again—there were matters to discuss with her. From the day she walked out on him and his lies, Sarah knew there was a gulf between what he said and what he meant. Over the intervening years, she got used to this, but every time she found Alex was departing from the truth, another nail dug into the coffin of their relationship.

She had made a pleasant life for herself away from New York but at heart she was a city girl, so had no desire to run off to some rural village to weave baskets or live through the Depression in abject loneliness and discomfort.

Alex might have lied about his involvement with his mistress and allowed his family to be put at risk as a result of his many dubious business activities, but he always ensured that she and the boys wanted for nothing of any material value.

By the time she arrived, Alex had ordered her a coffee with cream just how she liked it. This rankled with Sarah because it was down to her to decide what she wanted, but of course he had made the correct decision.

"Thanks for agreeing to see me, Sarah."

"That's okay. You're still the father of my children and we love them enough to want what's best for them, right?"

"Why, yes."

"So I'm guessing this has something to do with them."

"Well, indirectly, for sure."

Sarah stared at him, unsure what he meant. If it wasn't the boys, what could they possibly have to chat about? Alex started by asking how she had been and small talk persisted for an interminable five or ten minutes. She did her best not to appear impatient because she knew he operated at his own, usually brisk, pace and did not appreciate being thrown off his plan. So she chatted and waited for the payoff.

"SARAH, I NEED you to know that I'm not seeing anybody."

"Thanks for telling me, but it is none of my business anymore, Alex. You see who you want and the same goes for me. We aren't together and haven't been for two years."

"Two long years."

"We've had our difficulties, but we're in a decent place now, don't you think?"

"Yes, Sarah, I do. And that's what I wanted to talk to you about today."

"I'm listening, but I have absolutely no idea what you're on about."

"Sarah." Alex put down his cup and peered directly into her eyes with so much intensity that she too placed her cup back on its saucer. "I've been working hard ever since you… we split up to get on the straight and narrow. To do the right thing. I have been successful in my business dealings and have set aside a reasonable amount of money. That's how I have been able to afford to keep myself in clover and to ensure you and the boys have been looked after properly."

"I appreciate the house, the maid and all the other things you have done for us. It hasn't gone unnoticed."

"I'm pleased, Sarah, but I want more."

Sarah laughed, "You haven't changed. You were never satisfied with anything you had."

"But that's my point. I believe I have changed. If you would do me the honor of getting back together with me, I would walk away from my enterprises. If that is what it required to get you to return, then that is what I would do."

Sarah placed her hands on her lap.

"I want you fully in my life, Sarah. I have missed you and I yearn for your company again."

Sarah said nothing and sipped from her drink. Now she wished she'd agreed to add a splash of gin.

"As I've told you before, Alex, it isn't what you do for work that meant I had to leave. I was a *nafka* when you met me and you were a slugger. A whore and a street thug were a perfect match, right?"

He allowed a smile to erupt out of the corner of his mouth and then his lips subsided back to the usual countenance.

"You make money the only way you know how and I accepted that a long time ago—probably before we even got together. The problem I have with your work is that the people you deal with threatened the boys and me. I want to live in a world where my children can be safe. They should be able to go to bed and believe they will still be alive in the morning and not wind up riddled with bullets."

"For you I would quit the business—I've sufficient money as I said."

"Alex, you also know that isn't enough for me. When I left, there was one other thing that drove me away from you…"

"I don't see her anymore. I'm not seeing anybody."

"That was not the issue, Alex. The fact you'd slink out at night and spend time with that actress wasn't your finest moment, but I could have forgiven you. Your lying did us in the end. If I can't trust you to be honest with me, then we have nothing. Bupkis."

"Do you believe what I am saying to you?"

She sighed and shrugged.

"Now, of course you mean what you say, but that is not the issue for me. The question is whether you will still mean it this evening, tomorrow or any day in the future. That's what is so tough for me to accept. There have been too many times in the past when you have said all the right things and then done the opposite."

He swallowed hard.

"And, Alex, I would love to believe you. The idea we could make all this better between us would lift my heart. But do you mean it? Is Ida really in the past now? And would you give up your famous, dangerous friends just for me and the boys? I'm not seeing it, you know?"

"I'd do it in an instant if you'd really come back to me."

Sarah finished her coffee and dabbed her lips with her napkin.

"Let's leave things for now—give me a chance to think through what you have said. And it means we won't end in an argument. I know how you are when you don't get your way immediately."

She stood up and walked out of the diner, leaving Alex to stew on what she had declared and for his men to escort her to the waiting taxi.

March 1933

6

ALEX HAD FIRST met Charlie Lucky shortly after his arrival in the country, but they did not work closely together until after Alex's return from the Great War and his move away from his first mentor, Waxey Gordon and into the orbit of the Big Bankroll.

Now they were both members of the syndicate, an organization created by Charlie who acted as its chief executive. The Italian succeeded by thinking beyond the moment in which he lived. Tomorrow's problems were today's discussions, and this morning was no different.

"Alex, our world will change shortly and we need to be ready."

"I saw the papers too—they are giving up on Prohibition."

"The Protestant experiment had to end at some point and it looks like it is this month."

"So soon and so suddenly, Charlie."

"Don't sound too surprised. Any time such a dumbass idea ends up being law, you can bet it'll be repealed when everybody wakes up and smells the coffee. This was doomed before it began."

"We've made good money out of it though. I can't see honest folk visiting our speakeasies to buy watered down booze when they could pick up the real deal from some reliable Joe down the street."

"Alex, I reckon you're right, although we need to think what we will do with all that real estate. Sell it? Turn it into... I don't know what."

"We might not have all the answers now, but we'll figure it out. Besides, Roosevelt is signing the paperwork and it'll take several months before every state gives up on the whole sorry mess."

"There are enough individuals who dip their beaks in the trough who'll want it to last as long as possible."

"Yeah, Alex, there are sufficient cops and politicians on our payroll; it'll still be around until the end of the year."

"And at that point we require a fresh source of revenue."

"Correct, which is why I wanted to speak with you today."

"Go on, Charlie. I'm always interested in your plans, especially when we can both make some gelt along the way."

"Okay, this is the deal. I need not tell you how much green we've made from booze, but there's another commodity we must get into that'll make liquor money seem like chump change. And that is... heroin."

Alex's eyebrows rose toward the roof. Until now, he had known Charlie was importing the brown powder from North Africa using his connections in Sicily. Over the years, he had even helped his friend when the fella had the occasional transportation issues, but it was another thing to get involved directly.

"I don't know, Charlie."

"What's not to know? We buy the raw material through my friends in Palermo, ship it over here—we already have the transportation network thanks to moving all that Scotch and gin from Scotland and England—cut up the product with other powder and peddle it on the streets for a crazy profit."

"Heroin is different, Charlie."

"How is that, Alex?"

"We provide girls, we take bets, we sell liquor. Those are all things that men crave and whether or not we were there, they'd keep looking until they found them. But heroin... ordinary Joes don't need that stuff. We'd be selling them something they have no interest in. Do we really want our business to be based on forcing people to buy our goods? That sounds difficult to me and not what the politicians we have currently in our pockets will want to be involved in either. They'll run a mile from us when they find out."

Charlie looked at Alex all the while he spoke, a wry smile fixed upon his face. He let Alex say his piece and nodded occasionally to show he understood and respected his good friend.

"I understand your concerns, Alex. So tell me, do you like a pipe?"

"Not for a while. Haven't had a toke since Sarah left me. I went on a bender for a week and not a puff since."

"Alex, there's nothing wrong with an occasional opium pipe. The Chinese have been using them for generations, right?"

"Sure."

"But heroin is just processed opium. They are the same thing. If you are okay with opium pipes, then you shouldn't object to heroin. They are made from the same poppy."

Alex stared at Charlie and blinked. He hadn't thought about it that way before. He had no direct experience of heroin and didn't know anyone who used it, whereas the showbiz types who Ida mixed with always had a pipe in tow. Opium was normalized for him and heroin was something the Jews of Brooklyn did, but not the sophisticated guys in Manhattan.

TWO DAYS LATER, Alex found Charlie in his hotel suite and carried on where they left off.

"Why would we want to get involved in heroin trafficking when it's only in the last couple of years that the government has banned the stuff?"

"Alex, it is the law of supply and demand. If nobody wanted heroin, then there'd be no need to prohibit its use. Uncle Sam has basically announced to us that there's a business opportunity to seize."

"And if we don't do it...?"

"Some other guy will. You can bet your last dollar on that. So many fellas have the transportation infrastructure and distribution networks thanks to booze. Almost every syndicate member has the capability—and then there are guys in other parts of the country who could just as easily head east as any other direction. Either we find some other use for what we are sitting on or we start from scratch with I don't know what."

"I guess it's the same as the stuff they put in patent medicines."

"And who doesn't like a bottle of cola?"

"Or cough syrup."

"That's my point, Alex. The drug has been accepted for decades and now they are opening the floodgates on booze, they need something else to control people's lives over. Politicians are the worst. Pure scum. We should know because we bribe them enough."

They shared a chuckle, as they understood all too well how true that comment was. Alex fell silent for a spell, eyes cast downward, and felt Charlie watching him. When he looked up, he saw the guy's broad grin.

"So you in?"

"In principle. We haven't talked about gelt. If I move into the heroin trade, won't I have to give up on the Murder Corporation?"

"Not necessarily—at least not initially."

"Charlie, explain to me how I can have my cake and eat it."

"Well, I still need you to work with Albert and Louis. Albert might be a made man, but he nevertheless needs to listen to sensible advice —and he and Louis don't always see eye to eye."

"Okay…?"

"Bear with me. What I am proposing is that you and I go into business together, but as a side project, at least at first. You keep your current interests, as do I, and if I'm right, then we'll be awash with heroin money before the end of the year and can make some changes then. And if I am wrong, then we have lost nothing."

"Apart from our time, energy and investment capital."

"Yes, of course. But that's America, isn't it? You put your cojones on the line and see if you still have them in the morning."

"God bless America."

"Yeah, whatever."

"And will you inform the rest of the syndicate about our arrangement so everything is open, Charlie?"

"Why should we tell them about a private deal? It doesn't affect them and besides, the best way to kick-start a new venture is to keep it all small until you can expand. When we do, we'll cut in all our friends. If this thing is as big as I think it will be, then everyone dips their beaks in this trough and we'll need them to keep up with demand."

"Could it really get bigger than booze?"

"The profit we make? For sure. We watered down alcohol by ten or twenty percent. We'll dilute the heroin from Sicily by ninety-five percent. To my mind that makes it a better commodity because you can ship less across the Atlantic and still generate more money."

"With liquor, you take it from the boat, stack it in a warehouse and drive it to a bar. For heroin, don't you need somewhere to process the drugs and then a bunch of guys to hit the streets and sell the powder?"

"Right—and even with those extra costs, it's a better market to be in. Alex, you know I have worked this angle since the mid-twenties. Not in a big way, but I've been experimenting on how best to make this business work and I think I've found how to do it."

Alex looked deep into his friend's eyes. Charlie Luciano sure was enthusiastic over packets of brown powder, in a way he hadn't seen for a long time.

"Why me?"

"Alex, you have built up an impressive transportation network. Don't pretend Arnold didn't entrust you to create the principal route from Canada to New York for hard liquor. And you then protected it against other gangs, the cops, the Feds—the list goes on. You will have that transport system idle very soon and we can put it to excellent use. And if I haven't stroked your ego enough, I trust you, and you know how to handle yourself. I'll need a fella like you before this business is over."

He thought through all the angles and reckoned Charlie was right. Alex stuck out his hand and they shook to seal the deal.

7

ALEX HAD FORGOTTEN how old Ida looked—he hadn't seen her for months and the thought of her only appeared in his head the moment he disavowed her to Sarah. They had spent New Year together because he couldn't think of anything else to do and she had been available.

Despite the widening gulf between them, Alex continued to pay for her hotel accommodation and imagined that he always would. He felt no malice toward her—the truth was, he thought very little about her at all. That was the trouble. As much as he yearned for some form of companionship, Ida had stopped offering him that quite some time ago. Even before Sarah left, he had been talking of ditching the skirt, but had never been bothered enough to do anything significant about it.

Once or twice a month, he'd pop over and spend a night in her bed. A couple of years before, they had gone to the theater and he had spent time with her acting buddies, but those opportunities had fallen away.

Nowadays, they'd call room service for food, then Alex would satisfy himself with her, sleep, and leave before she woke. So Alex forgave Ida's surprise when he phoned and asked if she was free that evening.

HE OPENED THE door to the suite with the key he'd kept all these years and called out a quick hello.

"I'm in the bedroom. Make yourself a drink and I'll be with you in a minute," came the disembodied voice. He smiled and wandered through the hallway and dropped his coat on a nearby armchair.

"You want something?" he bellowed but received no reply. A shrug and Alex pulled out a bottle of Scotch from a closed sideboard. Ida hid the bottle because Prohibition was still in force in New York and she wanted no trouble from inquisitive maids. Two cubes of ice in the glass and he dropped onto one end of the couch.

She left him waiting for countless minutes before appearing in a red housecoat covering a pair of gold silk pajamas. For such a simple set of clothes, she had spent a ridiculous amount of time putting them on. She smiled as she rustled toward Alex and bent down to peck him on the lips before swishing round to fix herself a cocktail.

Once the cosmo was complete, Ida returned to the couch and sat next to him—all this while she had said not a word.

"Good to see you, Ida."

"Marvelous to see you too, darling."

"How have you been?"

"Oh you know how it is. I've been in between parts for so long now, I can barely remember my lines."

"I thought you were enjoying being the shining star on the cabaret circuit."

"Of course, my dear. Every week, there's somewhere I can sing. That meets my material needs—as well as your generosity, darling— but it doesn't feed my soul."

Alex listened to Ida's words and believed very few of them. By the time they dated, she was washed up, which was why she was taking jobs in upmarket speakeasies and not spending all her days in the Yiddish theater. There was nothing about her subsequent lifestyle that would have endeared her to off-Broadway producers.

They settled in and sipped their drinks. He listened to her reminisce about her glory days and Alex shared what little he was prepared to say about his business dealings and associates. While they chatted, he couldn't decide if he'd had enough of this woman or whether he wanted to grab her by the hand and take her to the bedroom. His ambivalence was difficult to measure.

"Then Larry took me to one side and whispered into my ear as he cupped my breast to tell me that the chicken feathers had left the room…"

Ida lived in the past and Alex was more concerned with what lay ahead in the world, but, she offered him the comfort of knowing what he was like and making so few demands of him that she was barely noticeable altogether. He blinked and focused on the curves of her body again—at least the ones visible through her housecoat. Despite the ravages of the intervening years, she still created flutters in the pit of his stomach. No other woman apart from Sarah could make that claim, other than Rebecca, whom he'd dated only a couple of times before the war.

Not that he had only slept with those three women—in fact, he'd not even got to first base with Rebecca. But there had been many others he had shared a bed with. Whenever he hit the nightclubs, a gaggle of girls would beat a line to his table, dropping handkerchiefs for him to pick up, or just walking straight up to him and starting a conversation.

Sometimes, he would invite the prettier ones to join him and on other occasions, he would feign ignorance and let them pass in the night. These conquests didn't mean much to him and he felt that was his problem. No woman could give him what he wanted—safety for the future and a calm place to sleep in the evening.

IDA STOOD UP to get herself another drink. "Want another?"

"I'm good, thanks. Why don't you throw on something warmer and we could go out for a meal?"

"Really, darling? I thought we might enjoy the rare moment we spend together nesting here."

"Ida, I thought we could try that new restaurant that's opened up opposite Lindy's. Then I reckon there'd be enough time to catch a show."

"I'd prefer to nest, Alex, but if you really need to be surrounded by other people, then let's go out to eat, but I have no desire to watch some hack annihilate a playwright's work. Even a second-rate writer deserves better than what's on offer on Broadway nowadays."

"I've read that theatreland is filled with Yiddish stars performing their old shtick for a *goyishe* crowd. I suggested it because I thought you might know some of the hoofers."

"Dear Alex, you are sweet, but really any of my peers has left the mainstream years ago. I mean to say, the travesty that calls itself theater is not worth even a cursory glance."

Alex sighed. This is what Ida was like. When she wound herself up on a topic, there was almost no way to talk her down from her high horse.

"Ida, it was only a suggestion. Forget about a show, but let's at least escape this place and go to a restaurant for some fine dining."

"There was a point when the only thing you'd want to do was to beat a retreat to my bedroom and never fly."

"And there was a time, Ida, when you had fire in your belly and a love of the crowd. Those days are gone, wouldn't you say?"

"We've all got older, Alex. That's all. Times change and you have to either accept the new ways or rail against them."

"Seems to me that you've done neither. Instead you're clinging to the banks of the river and hoping that everything will plain sail away. It's why you don't like leaving this suite I pay for."

"Let me go and change, Alex, before the conversation turns too acrid."

He had no idea what that meant and knew she was smarting from what he had said—Ida used difficult words whenever she wanted the upper hand. She knew he'd done little book work back in the old country and absolutely none after he arrived in America—unless you counted learning English when he was in base camp before he went off to fight.

IN GROSSMANN'S RESTAURANT, Alex had secured a table near the window because he knew Ida would enjoy the attention from an occasional passerby. He booked the spot just after Ida agreed to get dressed and when he was initially told they had no places free that evening, he explained he was Alex Cohen and wondered if the maître d' would be kind enough to check the bookings again.

"This is a delightful place—I'm glad you persuaded me to try it."

Ida's chin appeared briefly above the menu and he caught a smile. Alex always could make her head spin by spending gelt. Despite her bold thespian flourishes, Ida was a simple girl at heart who would follow the glitzy and shiny things until the end of the world.

"They say the steak is very good, but I doubt if there's anything abominable on offer."

"I'd prefer some grilled fish. Will that be a problem?"

"Shouldn't be. You ask and if the waiter kicks up a fuss, then let me handle the situation, but he won't."

Ida picked up the frosty edge in Alex's voice with his last few words. Her smile vacated her face for a second until she forced it to return. This was a dangerous man to cross and she knew it all too well.

Alex ordered two gin coffees with their meal and wondered if he would ever regain a taste for wine. Since Prohibition had started, there had been bottles of champagne to consume with his friends, but nothing as simple as a bottle of red to go with a bowl of pasta. He laughed to himself—he was becoming more Italian by the day. *Lokshen* soup and a glass of white—that'd be better.

In the taxi on their way to Ida's hotel, she got fresh with him, but he wasn't interested. The alcohol coursing through her veins was making her frisky, whereas the same liquor inside Alex made him want to withdraw from the world in reaction to her hotter advances.

When they got back to the suite, she responded to being spurned by ignoring him and stripping off in a last-ditch attempt to attract him to her. When that didn't work, the only thing left for Ida to want was her pipe. Alex walked out as she lapsed into a stoned silence as the opium fumes reached the depths of her lungs.

8

THE NEXT MORNING, Alex sat with Albert and Louis in a nondescript second floor office in Brownsville. The other two spent much of their time in this place, but Alex was far from comfortable. If he ignored the fact he had to leave Manhattan, then he was stuck with the peeling wallpaper and the ever-present sense that roaches could crawl out of the skirting board at any moment.

Albert offered the other two men a cup of coffee which they both accepted and only once he had settled back into his chair did matters progress.

"We have a contract to carry out."

"What's the story, Albert?"

"Looks like a young guy has overstretched his reach and whacked a fella without due authority, Louis."

"And did the fella survive?"

"No, Alex. This a hit and we should ensure the guy knows what has happened to him before he dies."

"So let's ask Abe to find a local gun to get this matter sorted."

This was a simple plan—Abe Reles was a reliable fella who had a vast network of contract killers. Sometimes Alex thought the whole of Brownsville must be stuffed with assassins, but he knew there were some ordinary citizens somewhere in the area.

"Good idea, Louis, other than the hit needs to happen in Atlantic City."

"Don't we have any contacts who could sort this out for us?"

"Why don't we just save ourselves the hassle, Albert, and I'll pop over tomorrow and get the job done."

"If you're sure, Alex."

"I fancy a day by the sea, so why not?"

ALEX STOOD ON the main boardwalk in Atlantic City as water droplets from the sea mingled with his hair. There was something refreshing about being battered by the wind next to a beach.

While he'd said he was looking forward to a day out, this was not entirely true. What he really wanted was to grab a break from his beloved New York. The city kept him alive, but it felt like it was dragging him down—his women troubles and the threat of losing all he had earned thanks to the onslaught of Prohibition weighed heavily on his shoulders.

Hands in pants pockets, Alex wandered along the wooden slats, passing diners, casinos, and other places of ill repute, all of which were owned by syndicate member, Enoch Johnson. The reason Alex was in town was because of Enoch's complaint against smalltime hood, Ziv Quigley, a mixed-race mongrel with an Irish father and Jewish mother.

This was not why Enoch had raised an issue with the syndicate. His beef was with the way the boy comported himself around town. Specifically, Ziv would often be heard badmouthing his boss, Enoch, in the late-night drinking establishments where the guy held court.

Ziv boasted about the money he was making—no sin in being proud of your own success—and of how he was skimming from the take at the casino where he worked. This was two mistakes rolled into one. First, he shouldn't have been doing it at all and, second, don't tell people you're stealing from your boss, especially when he is a member of the syndicate.

Alex continued his promenade until he reached the last storefront but one before the wooden walkway vanished into the sand of the beach. He looked up and down to check nobody was paying him any attention and entered the nearest building, The Lucky Nugget.

On arrival, he was greeted by a young woman who took him to the bar so he could buy a coffee before being shown through a curtained door and into a gaming room filled with a mix of roulette wheels and card tables. Alex judged the lay of the land by playing a few hands of blackjack.

He had a rudimentary description of Ziv and the rest he would make up as he went along. Just by chance when Alex entered the room, most of the baize counters had female dealers so he headed to a young male, who was the likeliest candidate of all the current crop of people running the card games.

A few hands later and Alex was twenty bucks up—at the expense of the two others sat at the table. One folded and stood up to find a luckier dealer and the other guy swapped out more green hoping the fortune of the cards would change just because he wanted it to.

Alex carried on hitting and sticking almost randomly to see what happened and, sure enough, he continued to win–he knew he was being played by the dealer. Alex glanced at the name badge on the guy's chest and read: Z Quigley. He'd found his mark.

He let the game carry on until he figured out all of Ziv's moves. The boy had practiced well, but a keen eye could see when he was palming and dealing from the bottom of the deck. Ziv didn't do it every time he supplied a card, but several times a round—and consistently so. They reached a point where Alex was now losing more than he was winning.

"Lady Luck has slipped off my shoulder."

"Never mind, Mac. I'm sure she'll come back and visit ya."

The accompanying chuckle had an edge to it that made Alex think Ziv was a little too cocksure. He smiled but let the rest of the hands play out and when his gelt ran out, he decided there was no need to feed the boy any more notes.

"I'm out and off to the bar. Can I get you anything?"

"Mighty upright of you. An Irish coffee would certainly hit the mark—if that's not too big an ask."

"Sure thing. And call me Alex."

He walked off to find the drinks and returned a minute later to hover near the edge of the action as though he was enjoying the scene. Thirty minutes afterward as the final john left the table, leaving Ziv with no customers, Alex struck up a conversation with the lad who had stolen fifty bucks from him already.

"You aware of anywhere else a guy can play cards?"

"What do you mean, Alex?"

"I was wondering if there were private tables for people who have a little more money to wager."

"You one of them guys, Alex?"

"I reckon so, Ziv. You know of any private gaming in this town?"

Ziv stopped tidying up his station and stared into the barrel of both Alex's eyes. In that split second of judgment, Ziv sealed his fate.

"There's a hotel suite nearby where high rollers can go, but you need an invitation."

"Would you be able to get me in, Ziv? I'd sure appreciate it."

Alex smiled and flashed a note between his knuckles so Ziv understood there was money to be made by hooking Alex up.

"Stay there and let me see what I can do, Alex. I won't be long."

In the time it took Ziv to go to the lobby, place a call and return to the table, Alex had picked out at least three other dealers who were palming cards. He ignored that issue and followed Ziv out of the Lucky Nugget and away from the boardwalk.

ZIV LED ALEX two blocks along the street and then ducked into an alleyway. Although he was only ten feet behind the boy, Alex couldn't see quite what was around the corner and knew to be ready.

As he turned into the alley, Ziv was visible at the far end—perhaps he was straighter than he appeared. Alex caught up with him and grabbed Ziv by the sleeve.

"What's with the rear entrance?"

"Let's just say that the fellas at the front won't welcome a guy like you to a game like this."

"But the players will be all right?"

Ziv blinked twice before answering.

"Yeah, they are stand-up guys in the room. It's just the goons in the lobby aren't too welcoming of strangers."

Alex knew that anyone dumb enough to follow Ziv into an alleyway was sufficiently stupid to believe his nonsense, but he carried on walking behind the boy as they entered the back of the building at the end of the alleyway.

Down a corridor and into the kitchen of what looked like a hotel—some of Ziv's story was true, then. Out of the cooking area and off to a service elevator and up to the sixth floor. By now, Alex was intrigued to find out with what action Ziv had got himself involved.

Ziv patted Alex on the shoulder when he explained to a suit on the door that this stranger was with him. The goon checked Alex for weapons and found nothing, so they stepped aside and allowed him in.

Much to Alex's relief, he didn't recognize anybody—all local guys, but judging by the color of the chips, they were all high rollers; the pot held at least ten thousand when they walked in.

Ziv introduced the assembled throng to Alex and he waited for Alex to show his appreciation before sitting down at the back of the room. Gaming etiquette demanded Ziv hang around for a while so as not to mess with anyone's concentration.

Alex also stuck to the side of the room until he was invited to join the table. He swapped out a bundle of green for chips and played out at least a dozen hands. The game was straight and he created some inroads into profit, but he needed to keep some of his attention on Ziv.

Sure enough, two hours later the boy prepared to leave. Alex apologized and explained that his losses meant he should quit before he was in too big a hole. He had ensured he'd slowly lost ground after his earlier good fortune.

He and Ziv took the same route out of the joint as they'd entered and they closed the door to the alleyway on their way out.

"Wait a minute, I've got something in my shoe."

Alex feigned trying to balance on one foot and beckoned for Ziv to stand near so he could lean on the boy and sort out his footwear. As soon as the kid had positioned himself as Alex's resting post, he pulled out a shiv from his ankle that the goon hadn't even bothered to check properly and stuck it deep into Ziv's stomach.

The boy fell to the ground in an instant and Alex towered over him, looking to the entrance of the alleyway in case some nosey citizen looked the wrong way in that instant. Nobody. Alex bent down and removed the blade from Ziv's gut. Blood gushed out— Alex was careful not to be on the receiving end of the mess.

"Listen to me. I have a message from Enoch Johnson: do not steal from him. Do you understand?"

Ziv couldn't verbalize his response but attempted to nod amid his whimpering. Alex grabbed the boy's right hand and sliced a finger clean off.

"No one likes a thief," he hissed as he slashed Ziv's throat wide open. Before he left A.C., Alex popped back to the Lucky Nugget and asked to speak with the manager.

9

THE SYNDICATE RARELY met as an entire group, but the senior members would get together to discuss important matters as the need arose. With the demise of Prohibition on the horizon, this was one such time and a private room at the Waldorf Astoria had been reserved in a fictitious name. Charlie chose the venue in remembrance of Rothstein's New Year parties, but frivolity was far from the minds of the attendees.

Along with Charlie and Alex were Meyer Lansky and Benny Siegel. Meyer had positioned himself as the primary financier for the group, always eager to have several fingers in as many different pies as he could manage. He wasn't the Big Bankroll, but he had gained sufficient financial acumen thanks to the profits generated by bootlegging and his other illegal pursuits.

Benny was the flightiest of the group, but he was not to be underestimated. A steely yet impatient figure, he had gained a reputation as a killer and cemented that with his focus on gaming operations in Manhattan and Brooklyn. Before it had a formal name, Benny had worked with Charlie to set up Murder Corporation and continued to take contracts when they were big enough to warrant his attention.

The men sprawled across a number of easy chairs, reminiscent of their times in Arnold's apartment. Alex had known them for over a decade and they were comfortable in each other's company. Meyer and Benny had been friends since childhood—Charlie had done business with Lansky when they were teenagers.

"There's only one thing I want us to talk about and that is the impending demise of our bootlegging operations."

"Charlie, we need to figure out what we will do with the trucks, the warehouses and the speakeasies."

"Benny, you are right that we will need to dismantle what we have in place, but more important is to work out where we go from here. When the booze money dries up, we will still have men who expect to get paid and who will want to dip their beaks in the trough."

Charlie nodded at Alex's words, as they all did, but there was little consensus on where next. Meyer was the first to break the silence.

"Perhaps we just need to do more of what we do. We should also check our profit margins. Shaving a few cents here and there will make a substantial difference to our bottom line."

"Spoken like a true accountant."

The group chuckled as Meyer scowled at Benny's quip, who realized he may have overstepped the mark.

"I mean, you are correct, Meyer. We must certainly improve on the money we make on existing ventures, but I doubt if we'll replace all the bootlegging revenues that way. Right, Charlie?"

"Damn straight. We need something new. Yes, we must keep everything ticking over, but that won't be sufficient. The good news is that we are not alone. Everyone is in the same boat and we are all looking around to find the next big thing. We just need to be the first to get there."

"Whoever is in early gets to control the business."

"Right, Meyer. Spoken like a true businessman."

Smiles all round as Charlie echoed Benny's words, but without the edge.

THE FELLAS TOOK a break to order in some food and to grab yet another coffee. This also gave everybody a chance to chat among themselves. The mix of pasta and latkes appeared strange on the table but nobody commented as they had all ordered precisely what they wanted and each individual was too powerful to be questioned on their culinary decisions by any member of the waitering staff.

"Anyone heard how Alfonse is getting on behind bars?"

"Not me, Charlie. Amazing how they managed to hit him without raising a fist."

"You're right, Meyer. It was the lack of paperwork that did him in. He had no evidence to show the prosecution were lying."

"What would you have done, Benny?"

"If I didn't have the receipts, then I'd have created them. Given what the Feds could have taken into court, a small amount of falsification of evidence would have been nothing."

Alex pondered the rights and wrongs of the situation. Charlie had cabinet after cabinet filled with a record of every legitimate purchase he'd ever made—along with some others which were still tax deductible should the need arise.

In contrast, Alex followed the Rothstein model and kept all the details in his head and nowhere else. The solitary filing cabinet in his study was singularly empty—a piece of office furniture only used to store an occasional bottle of Scotch.

"Charlie, do you think I should keep records?"

"Alex, why start now? Besides, if they ever come calling, I've got enough receipts to sink a battleship—you can always borrow a couple of crates of mine."

Benny laughed out loud and Meyer sniggered briefly, but Alex knew that Charlie was serious. Without receipts you lose because you can't defend yourself. With paperwork it shows you how much tax you should have paid and Uncle Sam calculates the size of your illicit earnings, so you lose. Neither option was great and both would send you straight to the slammer.

Alex considered another aspect of the situation, "The difference between Alfonse and those of us in this room is that he courted publicity. Most here are shy of the press."

"Don't look at me," intoned Charlie, "because the last thing I want is newspaper attention. My problem is that my name has become associated with a bunch of unsavory characters."

They laughed at that remark as he looked around the room and eyeballed each of them. While Charlie wasn't as brash as Alfonse had been, he still gave the occasional interview or comment if a member of the press came calling. Meyer refused to say anything on the record and Benny, along with Alex, was unknown outside of his personal circle.

To clear his head, Alex walked down to the lobby with the excuse of buying a packet of cigarettes, even though he knew he could call down for someone to bring them up to him.

ON THE FIRST floor, Alex bought his smokes and lit one before dropping into a nearby armchair in the hotel lobby. He was worried about what would happen to him and his friends. If the Feds were prepared to take Alfonse down, then it was only a matter of time before they came after Charlie and the rest of the group.

He took an enormous drag on his cigarette and watched the plume of exhaled smoke hang in the air above his head until it dissipated, while he pondered Charlie's heroin smuggling proposition again. If not opium, then where were they going to make their money?

Back up with the fellas, Alex had a suggestion: "Unless any of us can conceive of a fresh business line, we must do more than just squeeze what we've got left once we lose booze."

"What are you saying?"

"Meyer, it's not that you were wrong to think like an accountant. We should be more forensic than that. If prostitution has been good for us, then we must find new ways to generate money out of the oldest profession. Same with narcotics, gaming, and union bashing."

"Okay, so why don't we each take one of them and come back at the end of the month with some concrete approaches to double profit."

They all nodded in agreement to Charlie's proposal, in part because they all felt there would be no lightbulb moment. Before Prohibition started, none of them could have predicted how much gelt they would have made out of it. The smart ones saw that selling liquor would be good as the old bars went out of business, but only Arnold Rothstein envisaged how they could industrialize the transportation, storage, and distribution of the product to make some healthy money out of the Protestant desire for the purity of their souls.

Meyer volunteered to focus on the unions, Benny took gaming, and Charlie put his name down against narcotics, so that left Alex with the short straw. The oldest profession was also the one where most people had spent much time finessing into the streamlined factories that made up most cathouses. Nonetheless, he agreed to find fresh ways to generate new gelt out of old nafkas.

10

ALEX SPENT HIS life traveling from one diner to the next, a nomad in New York. He used to have a base in a seemingly innocuous office block downtown, but after too many attacks on himself and his family, Alex gave up on that and decided to only see business associates in public locations.

As for his friends, he would meet them in the privacy of their homes or hotel suites—whatever was most appropriate and the same was true for Sarah. With her, the problem was more that she tried to avoid meeting him at all and preferred to let the boys act as a social barrier between them.

He knew there must be something serious to discuss when she asked if they could meet up and offered to go into the city to make the schlep more convenient for him. So they sat opposite each other in Lindy's, which was as good a choice as any other joint in Manhattan.

Although he arrived some fifteen minutes early, Sarah was already there at their booth. She smiled briefly when she saw him and maintained that positivity in her expression until he sat down and ordered a coffee and some cheesecake.

"Thanks for seeing me, Alex."

"You're welcome. I'm surprised you were prepared to come all the way into the city just to see me. I hope you had some other errands to do today too."

"Sure, yeah…"

Sarah's eyes dipped down to her Key lime pie, which she mushed round her plate with a fork. Her hesitation piqued Alex's interest—she usually said exactly what she thought to him without batting an eyelid.

"Did you get here okay?"

"Yes, thanks."

"And are the boys all fit and well, Sarah?"

"I got the maid to keep an eye on them today. They are perfectly safe."

"Good. I wasn't trying to imply they weren't—just asking as a pleasantry, as their father. I know you always have their best interests at heart every waking moment."

Sarah switched on a smile again, but it flicked off almost as soon as it formed. Alex waited because whatever needed to be said was stuck in the back of her throat.

He settled into the seat and consumed three forkfuls of cake. It was perfectly baked and the base had a crunch to it. Every mouthful reminded him of Arnold and the rear table where he'd held court for so many years.

"We haven't been together for quite a while now, Alex."

"I know. I drove you away from me with my behavior and my not confronting the truth."

"You lied to me, yes, but I'm not trying to start an argument with you, so you shouldn't feel the need to defend yourself. That's not why I wanted us to meet up."

"Then what is the reason, Sarah?"

She took a glug of her drink, inhaled, and spoke, all the while gripping the cup as though it might fly away at any minute.

"Like I said, we have been living apart for over two years and I think it would be sensible for both of us if we were to, you know, make it official."

"Official?"

"Get the paperwork to catch up on our lives."

She looked right at him, not understanding his lack of comprehension. For Sarah had rehearsed this conversation in her head so many times, she thought she had imagined exactly how it would play out, but she had forgotten that Alex was incredibly smart in business but really dumb with women.

"The paperwork. What paperwork?"

"I've been speaking with a lawyer who says I should ask you if you'd agree to a divorce."

"We've only been separated for a brief time and, besides, I thought we might get back together…"

His voice trailed off—as soon as the words left his mouth, Alex realized how foolish they sounded even to him.

"Alex, it has been two long years and we are no nearer reconciling now than the day I walked out on you. I don't mean to sound harsh —it's just how it is, right?"

"I guess so… yeah. From that time I thought you would change your mind and come back to me at some point. I dunno. I suppose I just assumed."

"Well, Alex. I can't see that happening and I think it would be best for all of us if you agreed to divorce me. We could go to Reno for a few weeks perhaps."

"Spend six weeks away from business?—not now."

Even Alex knew New York had stringent divorce laws which required Sarah to provide evidence of his adultery. Clearly she figured this would be easier with his cooperation than without, especially as he hardly spent any time with his mistress and was too discreet to be seen out and about with a girlfriend. A trip to Nevada was common nowadays as that state would let you divorce if you were resident for a handful of weeks.

"Will you at least think about it some more, please? It's what's best for us all."

"So you keep telling me. I'll consider your request—you are the mother of my children and I respect you greatly—but I can't pretend to like the idea. Just one thing—are you seeing anybody?"

Sarah's cheeks reddened for a second. "Why no. This isn't about me but what's the proper thing to do for the boys."

◆ ◆ ◆

THE NEXT DAY, Alex met up with Ezra and Massimo back at Lindy's. This time he positioned himself in a rear booth facing the front. The red in Sarah's cheeks raised a query mark in his head.

"I have a job for one of you, but it involves Sarah, so I understand if you don't want to touch it."

Both men shifted uncomfortably in their seats—they were fiercely loyal to their boss but had also seen his relationship with her in the best and worst of times. Neither wanted to stand between the man and his wife. Ezra broke rank first.

"If you think I can help..."

"I may be paranoid but there's something I want you to check up on for me. Massimo, as this is a discreet matter, you need not stick around for the next part of the discussion."

The Italian shrugged, swigged back his coffee and slunk off, wishing he had been faster to respond, but he knew Alex felt no ill will toward him. That's not how the guy operated.

With Massimo near the door, Alex leaned forward, lowered his voice, and spoke directly to Ezra, staring at him throughout the rest of their conversation.

"I think Sarah might be having an affair and I want you to find out if that is true."

"An affair? You haven't lived together since..."

The truth was it had been so long, Ezra couldn't place the last time the two of them had slept under the same roof.

"...the first syndicate meeting. That was when she left me."

"I don't know how to ask my next question without making you angry."

"There are no secrets between us."

"Do you really think she's sleeping with someone else because you said you might be paranoid."

"I'm not too sure. When we spoke yesterday, she hesitated and looked embarrassed at only one point. She's not a person to feel ashamed, so..."

"I see. Let me have a dig around and see what I turn up."

"Find out all you can, but do nothing to the man—if there is a guy to do anything to. It's facts I am looking for, not some foolish revenge on a stranger."

"I understand. Once I've gone fishing, I shall report back to you but I will not share with Massimo. This is private between you and I."

"Damn straight. We live together, we love together…"

"…but we die alone."

TWO WEEKS LATER, Ezra met up with Alex at his favorite booth in Lindy's. He sat still while his boss fussed about the menu and ordering coffee and cake. After the displacement activity came the inevitable question: "What did you find out, Ezra?"

"Short answer: you were right, there is another man. How much do you want to know about him?"

"Tell me what you got."

"He's a lawyer; works in a local firm in Hoboken. Lives around the corner and has spent nights over with your wife."

"Does he spend time alone with my boys?"

"Sarah has gone out and left them with him."

Alex sighed and sipped from his cup. Ezra moistened the inside of his mouth because he knew this was far from over. He cleared his throat, "Would you like me to kill him?"

"Oh no. This is personal, not business. There's no need for him to die—not at my instigation at least."

"Whatever you say."

"Besides, if he were to meet an untimely end then Sarah would immediately suspect me and I would never be forgiven. How long has he been in her life?"

"Six months. That's when they started going steady and he stayed over with her."

"The boys have said nothing to me. Zilch."

"And now they spend two to three days a week together plus weekends."

Alex ground his molars and ceased listening to Ezra's comments. Lost in his thoughts, Alex vowed not to give that woman her divorce. While he had hoped they might get back together at some point, the one thing he was certain about was that if he couldn't have her then no other man would have her either. If they wanted each other that much, they could skulk around until the day they died. Then Alex mulled over the irony that Sarah was dating a lawyer.

"I should have the guy disbarred."

11

WITH THOUGHTS RICOCHETING around his head about Sarah and her paramour, Alex did his best to focus on the job at hand—a trip to Detroit on company business and a chance to speak with Abe Bernstein, the boss of the Sugar Hill gang. They'd worked with each other since the start of Prohibition and had profited greatly from each other's endeavors.

On this occasion, Alex popped over to the City of Champions with Ezra and Massimo. Sat in their private compartment at the rear of the train, the three men could have a comfortable ride without interference from any Joe citizen. Alex lost himself inside his own thoughts for most of the journey while the other two played pinochle. Luckily for his fellas, Alex was totally in focus by the time they arrived at Abe's joint to talk business.

"Good to see you, Abe. I hope you remember Massimo and Ezra."

"How could I forget either of these mensches from our glory days bootlegging and hauling liquor across the country?"

"Well said. With a bit of luck those happy days will return to us shortly."

Abe spat three times for luck, as was the Jewish superstition.

"Please God next year in Jerusalem," he intoned, although none of the men assembled in the back of the speakeasy had any desire to travel to the Middle East any time soon. This was just a saying passed down from the older generation to the following one, which had lost its meaning along the way.

"So to business, Abe. I don't need to tell you we are here with a contract and we are seeking your cooperation in this matter."

"And you shall have it, Alex, of course. One of my men stole from a syndicate member when he was on a trip to Little Italy and that is unacceptable."

"Can you give us an itinerary so we can find this thief?"

"I'll do one better than that and arrange for you to meet him. Name the location and we shall send him there within the hour. I don't want this *schnook* to walk the streets any longer than he has to."

"Abe, I admire your sentiment and desire to see justice done, but we have been sat on a train for I've forgotten how long. Would you mind if we rested a while first and had a meal without the table shaking and our forks wobbling in front of our faces with the movement of the carriage on the tracks?"

"Sorry, I forgot. The *gonif* can wait. You fellas relax and we will deal with the *meeskait* tomorrow. Would you like any companionship tonight?"

Both Ezra and Massimo expressed interest with a simple nod of the head and Alex shrugged, not sure whether he cared about his answer.

Abe took the four men to a family-run restaurant where they had all the Yiddish cooking comforts. Once they had finished their meal and returned to their hotel, three women were waiting in the lobby for them.

"Which one would you like, Alex?"

"You two take whoever you want and I'll have what's left."

"Sure?"

"Yes, Ezra. I really don't care."

THE BRUNETTE FOLLOWED Alex into the elevator and read the situation well. Her girlfriends were pawing Ezra and Massimo before the doors slammed shut to take them up to the fifth floor, but Alex's broad stood near him without touching. She let her hand float toward his, but picked up on the fact that he wasn't grabbing and mauling her like his companions.

In his suite, she sat down on a couch as Alex sloped into his bedroom to put away his overcoat. Realizing he hadn't been followed, he popped his head round the door of the living room.

"Do you have a name, doll?"

"What do you want to call me?"

"Rebecca. And if you are going to earn any money tonight, I think you should join me."

A brief smile flickered across her face as she rose and headed toward him. When she neared him, Alex turned and walked back to the bedroom and on to the en suite bathroom. Just before he brushed his teeth, he muttered instructions for Rebecca to get into bed, which she dutifully obeyed.

He undressed and slipped under the sheets, aware of Rebecca's body for the first time. In the elevator, he hadn't bothered to pay her much attention but now, up close, he saw she was an attractive woman. Ezra and Massimo had left the best for last—for him.

He switched off the bedside light, curled into a ball with his back to the nafka and Rebecca spooned him until he fell asleep. In the morning, he placed a wad of green in her purse and thanked her for her understanding.

NOY YARDEN HAD been given a simple task by Abe Bernstein—to visit Little Italy, collect a package and return home with no fuss. Abe gave him sufficient funds to afford to stay in a reasonable hotel overnight and to keep himself in clover while in the Big Apple. Noy traveled coach on the train and negotiated his way across town until he arrived on Mulberry.

This was when a tiny error of judgment on his part created a massive difference to his life chances, because he took most of his remaining funds and used them to get into the back room of a nearby speakeasy. Emboldened by the ease with which he gained access to the high stakes game, Noy tried an all-or-nothing strategy.

He pulled out a gun and stole all the money that was on the table and anything lying inside the patrons' wallets. Then Noy did the only sensible thing and scarpered, picked up the package and headed straight for the station and the first train to Detroit.

Within ten minutes of this happening, and several hours before Noy arrived back home, Abe received a call from Johnny Torrio explaining that one of his men had just entered a Torrio gaming house and committed grand larceny. The following day, Johnny asked permission from the syndicate to whack Yarden and the guy's fate was sealed with a unanimous verdict. Nobody likes a thief, especially other thieves.

ALEX, MASSIMO, AND Ezra paid a visit to Noy to check on his welfare. He answered the door of his apartment wearing his pants and a tee shirt. He looked like he'd thrown the clothes on straight from getting out of bed, although it was late morning by the time they'd had breakfast and headed over to Noy's pad.

"Noy Yarden?" inquired Alex.

"Who wants to know?"

"We're friends of Abe's. Didn't he mention we might visit?"

"Nah, but he doesn't tell me everything. Come in and give me two minutes to get dressed."

"You got company, kid?"

Alex asked the question with a light air to his voice, but Ezra glanced at Massimo as the answer was given. A dame in the place would add an unnecessary complexity to their day.

"Not this morning, Mac."

"You kick her out early?"

Massimo grinned at the implication that Noy was a player, but maybe the Italian tried a little too hard or perhaps the three men gave off a suspicious air. Whatever the reason, Noy looked between them all and bolted back inside. Massimo chased him and Ezra pelted down the stairs because he thought he'd spotted Noy glance at the fire escape in his bedroom through the open living room.

Alex remained still, sighed, and sauntered into the apartment and closed the front door. At this point, Noy approached the bedroom window, flung the sash down and put one foot out onto the fire escape.

Massimo reached him in time to grab an arm, but Noy wriggled free and squeezed his body through the crack made by the window. With a thump and a dash, he scrambled down the fire escape. Massimo banged and scratched at the window until the gap was big enough for him to fit through.

Meanwhile Ezra stormed down the central stairway and reached the first-floor lobby in record time. He shot out of the entrance and looked left then right, trying to see if Noy had reached the street.

With nothing to see and no one to chase, Ezra stood still, not certain what to do next. He craned his head up, hoping to spot Noy's apartment, but he wasn't even sure he knew which side of the building Noy's was facing. The answer fell from the sky twenty seconds later, when he appeared in the periphery of Ezra's vision about four hundred feet away as he landed on the sidewalk, having leaped from the fire escape ladder.

Ezra ran toward him and once Noy had stood up and seen Ezra lunging at him, he flew at full pelt in the opposite direction. Ten seconds later, Massimo appeared from the sky and joined Ezra as they sped to catch up with the lad.

Noy attempted to zigzag around the sidewalk, but there were too many people on the street to make that a quick journey. Thinking they couldn't see him, Noy ducked into an alleyway and the two men slowed down, knowing they had him trapped.

Massimo and Ezra strolled into the alley and watched as Noy tried to climb a wall at the far end. Massimo jogged over, grabbed a leg, and yanked the guy onto the ground. As soon as he landed, Ezra booted him in the kidneys to make sure he didn't get up.

Then Massimo kicked him twice—once between the legs and once in the head. While the first blow made Noy squeal, the second stopped him breathing and he lay still, one leg twitching in a death throe. They picked the body up and carried him over their shoulders as though he was drunk. On the street, they waited until a truck sped past and threw the carcass in front of the moving vehicle.

In the apartment, Alex had watched his lieutenants follow Noy into the alley. Then he turned his back on proceedings and walked through each room to ensure there was no evidence of their passing through the place. He pulled the door shut on his way out and met up with Massimo and Ezra before they left the vicinity and popped by Abe's before returning to New York.

12

BACK IN THE city, Alex spent some time with Ezra and Massimo thinking about how they could make more money out of prostitution, just as Alex had promised the fellas he would.

"We might force the nafkas to work harder and reduce the minutes they spend with the johns."

"Yes, Ezra, but I wouldn't say we encourage the men to hang around as it is—and if they do, we make them pay for it."

"Why not just double the number of working girls. Wouldn't that double profit?"

"More or less, but where would we get all these extra women and how would we afford to house and feed them?"

"Dunno, Alex."

Massimo knew his suggestion was far from perfect, but they were throwing ideas around and he reckoned it was as good as anything the others would come up with. The three men fell into silence for ten minutes or more as each tried to figure out a system to make even more money out of sex than they currently did.

"We should use high-class call girls and extort rich johns."

"Ezra, would you say that is in any way different from what we already do? When was the last time one of your nafkas refused to exploit the situation with a police captain or politician?"

"You're right, Alex. That's just business as usual."

"Expansion is a possibility, though, Ezra. If we either find some untrammeled territory or take over somebody else's patch…"

"Alex, the whole point of the syndicate was to stop that sort of thing from happening."

"Yes, Massimo. Back to the drawing board."

More silence and blank expressions, occasionally punctuated with a raised eyebrow when some bright idea sprung into a head, which would lower as the fella realized the flaw in the plan before he'd pitched it to the other guys.

"Booze was great because it came as part of a package. Johns would come to the speakeasy for a gin-soaked coffee and stay for the entertainment, play a few hands or try their hand at a roulette wheel…"

"…and if we were lucky, they'd nip upstairs for thirty minutes with a girl. Alex, without the lure of liquor, why will people come to our bars?"

"Good question, Ezra. Couples turned up for a show and a drink. Men appeared later in the evening and headed straight for the second floor."

"You think it was just being in the right place at the right time? There'll never be a moment like that again?"

"Maybe. I hope not, but perhaps. For now, we have to assume we can repeat that success once beer is no longer the bait to lure in the johns."

"Can I suggest the obvious, Alex?"

"I'm all ears, Massimo. No suggestion is too stupid, given what we've come up with this evening."

"Well, people enjoy a drink—that was why Prohibition was so great for us. And when it is legal, they will still want to knock back a beer or a shot of whiskey."

"Right."

"And men like to have sex."

Everyone chuckled and nodded.

"So why are we overthinking this? We keep the speakeasies open on the first floor and use the same locations for the nafkas on the second. That's what happened before Uncle Sam banned booze. It can be the same when they repeal the act."

Alex swallowed hard, looked at Ezra and back to Massimo, who grabbed at his glass and consumed the remains of his Scotch.

"Do you reckon we'll make as much money?"

"It'll be cheaper without having to bribe the cops or worry about security on the door."

"Good point, Massimo, although I guess some citizens liked to go to a speakeasy because it was criminal but not viewed in a bad way."

"Sure, perhaps there might be fewer drinkers, but that doesn't mean the volume of booze will reduce. Some people didn't trust the quality of our hooch. The joints were called blind pigs for a reason. They might consume more when they don't suspect the alcohol has been brewed in a bathtub."

Ezra tapped the table to attract the others' attention.

"I disagree—we'll see a big drop in the numbers coming to our drinking holes and should expect to close a stack of them down. But the ones that survive will make a load more gelt for us. Besides, when booze goes back to being legitimate, breweries will want a piece of the action and they'll get it. Perhaps the smartest thing is to let them in on the game."

"Why is that?"

"Alex, it's simple—when businesses move into an area, we provide them protection, offer to solve any problems they might have with any unions and sell them product. The way I see it: without Prohibition, it is business as usual, only with more opportunities than before because we have the capital to invest."

"Ezra, next thing you'll tell me to buy stock in General Motors."

"Not a bad plan, Alex. I might do that myself."

ALEX'S OLD FRIENDS gathered again at the rear of Linsky's—the same booth every time, no matter how short the notice of their arrival. Several lieutenants were rammed at the front of the restaurant to keep an eye on all the other patrons. Charlie, Meyer, Benny, and Alex relaxed over their coffees and cake.

"I've been trying to come up with something creative around prostitution, but it has not been easy, Charlie."

"I understand. Is there anything you have been able to think of to replace our lost profits?"

"We've played with loads of ideas but nothing will generate enough gelt to be worth talking about here—extortion of wealthy johns, protection money from businesses that move into our old speakeasy locations. These are the cream of the crop."

Benny laughed at the suggestions, knowing they wouldn't get close to the amount of money the fellas were seeking to make.

"And what's your bright idea, Benny?"

Benny cleared his throat and stared into Alex's eyes for dramatic effect.

"Gambling."

"I'm glad we're sat on these seats otherwise we'd have fallen on the floor, Benny. We are sitting in the midst of a genius, gentlemen."

"Less with the sarcasm, Alex. Benny, what are you proposing because we already have extensive gaming operations."

"Charlie, if we can't make more money here, we must go somewhere else to generate the gelt. It stands to reason and there are plenty of places where we have no foothold. We should go to one of them and repeat what we've done here but in new territories. We know what we need to do and we must search for the real estate where we can do it."

"And you think gaming is the answer?"

"Meyer, it is part of the answer and one of the easiest things to start from scratch. You give me a piece of green baize, a pack of cards and some chips. I'll have a casino up and running within a week."

"If it was that easy, every fool would do it. And before you get on your high horse, Benny, I'm not accusing you of being a fool—just saying that we both know it is more complicated than you state."

"Alex, no offense taken, but is it that difficult? If we have the strength of our own conviction, we could be raking in the money within a month."

The other three looked at each other. While they hadn't agreed with Alex, the men believed he was right. Gambling was a profitable enterprise for sure, but organizing a gaming house was complex if you wanted it to survive interest from the Feds, the cops, and other gangs—let alone managing the sort of john who rocks into a casino.

If they have any money on them worth taking then they need feeding and watering, along with tending to their other, more private needs.

"If the economy was in a better shape, then we could squeeze more out of the unions."

"Don't hold your breath, Meyer."

The conversation died again until Charlie spoke a minute later.

"There is an opportunity we have yet to examine, which promises to offer us substantial returns on our investment. It involves the importing of goods, for which we already have a significant transportation network. Then we need to repackage the item and sell it on the street. The profit margin is ten—a hundred—times bigger than liquor."

Alex could see the pay-off a mile away and wondered whether Charlie had pitched each of the men here with his private offer.

"Narcotics. I have contacts in Sicily who can obtain the heroin we'd need and we have enough warehouses going spare in the city. We could turn some of them into laboratories to cut the drug into something we could put on the streets. Then we use our fellas to move it at a vast profit."

"In the morning they deal with the numbers and in the evening they sell dope."

"That's the idea, Meyer."

"And do you think we'd keep the politicians we need for the rest of our activities?"

"Why not, Alex? Since when has Tammany Hall cared about anything other than who is lining their pockets and that their money keeps flowing? Provided they get their weekly payments, no politician will care what happens to a bunch of poor Jews and Italians."

"You think we should sell to our own, Charlie?"

"Yes, Benny. If we do this, we mustn't stray too far from what we know—at least not at the start. It'll be easier for us to keep control."

More cake and cups of coffee were consumed until all the details were ironed out. Only Benny seemed unconvinced about the power of heroin to save their asses—he continued to believe they should head west somewhere and pitch tent in a new location.

Midtown Huckster

13

ALBERT, LOUIS, AND Alex sat around a table in what was the closest thing to a board meeting of Murder Corporation. The three men had taken a position in a Mulberry Street restaurant at Albert's insistence.

"You should try the calamari marinara."

"I'm trying to avoid shellfish."

Albert smiled because he'd known this would be Alex's response. The Italian was just hoping to annoy him into reacting, but Alex was better than that. Louis remained silent and allowed the two others to play their games. He had learned to let Albert have his say and not to admonish him in public. The fella was quick to temper and liable to lash out without considering the implications of his actions.

"Contracts appear to continue to be flowing well and Abe Reles can still supply men for the jobs, right?"

"Sure thing, Albert. He's a good guy. I've been relying on him for years."

"That right, Louis?"

"Alex, he and I met years ago. I can't remember a point when I didn't know him."

"Same with you, Albert?"

"We go back some ways, but not as long as with Louis."

The waiter arrived to take their order and departed as quickly as he was able—he saw Anastasia, recognized Louis and was learning

Alex's face too. It had only taken him a couple of years, but to be fair to the guy, the three directors of Murder Corporation were more likely to meet midtown or out in Brownsville rather than in the heart of Little Italy.

"So, is there anything we should discuss?"

"Good question, Alex. There is one matter I'd like to raise."

"What's that, Albert?"

"We have been delivering what I can only describe as an excellent service to the syndicate and have done so from the moment we were formed. The three of us might not have conducted business together before then, but all has been running pretty smoothly between us ever since. Wouldn't you agree?"

"Yep."

Louis nodded, too.

"So one reason everything has been so peachy for us is that the rest of the syndicate has bought our services at a very reasonable rate."

"We agreed at the outset that there should be no bickering among ourselves over the cost of goods and services bought and sold between syndicate members."

"Yeah, Louis, but agreed by whom? I mean, did you negotiate the price we charge or did Luciano and Torrio impose that amount on us? Back in '29, that is."

"Shortly after the meeting in Atlantic City, we sat down and hammered out our fees."

"Alex, perhaps your head has got cloudy but I recall a price being named by Charlie and us nodding in agreement. There was no real negotiation—no discussion about the value of our services and the level of appreciation that would be shown for them. Just a number which we consented to with no other words being said."

"Albert, the conversation was brief, but I don't remember any of us feeling like we were being shortchanged."

"That's the difference between you and me then, Alex, because I maintain we are leaving money on the table and have done so from the time when the first contract was assigned to us."

Louis and Alex looked at each other and then turned their respective gazes on Albert, who stared both of them down. The man's mind appeared made up. Clearly this issue had been brewing for quite a while, but Alex had had no idea that Albert felt so aggrieved. Judging by Louis' expression, he was as surprised as Alex.

"Have you spoken to Charlie about this, Albert?"

"Not yet, because I wanted us to talk about it first."

Alex sighed because he had no desire to go behind Charlie's back on anything as important as this, but he also understood how powerful Albert was in the Italian gangs.

"What do you think, Louis?"

Alex figured the smart thing at this point was to throw the ball into Louis' court—he understood better than most how to handle Anastasia.

"I will never say that I don't want more money, Alex. And with all due respect to you, Albert, that doesn't mean I think now is the best time to broach this topic."

"You realize the syndicate has more pressing issues than giving us a price rise?"

"Alex, I'm pointing out that the end of Prohibition will throw up tremendous opportunities for us and that different gangs may well come into conflict with each other…"

"And we'll mop up the consequences of those disagreements?"

"Yeah. Chances are we shall make more money because there will be more bloodshed. If we ask for a bigger slice now, we might appear as though we are trying to have our cake and eat it. This may be true but it is not how we wish to appear, I would suggest."

Albert laughed and Alex smiled at Louis' remarks.

"This is why you and I have been friends for so long. I like the way you think, Louis Buchalter."

THE NEXT DAY, Alex made it his business to hook up with Louis in Brownsville. He predicted Buchalter would be more comfortable talking on home ground and that was what was necessary given the topic at hand.

"Do you reckon Albert is right to hike our prices?"

"There's nothing like getting straight to the point, Alex."

"I know but the look you gave me yesterday made me think you weren't keen on the idea and we should talk about it sooner rather than later. So, what are your thoughts?"

"I'm not sure my opinion counts for much."

"Don't be coy, Louis. There's only you and me here—you can be honest with me."

"Albert is a made man in the Italian mob—that means something much more than being a syndicate member. It's a Sicilian thing."

"Charlie has explained the inner workings of the Little Italy gangs to me. They have a deep sense of history and hierarchy. I get it and even if there was no syndicate, Albert would be a highly regarded and influential man, but do you think he is right?"

Louis looked into the middle distance and exhaled. Alex knew the conversation would be difficult, but he underestimated Louis' reticence—the man just didn't want to express an opinion out loud. Alex tried to give him the chance to consider his words carefully hoping something would come out of his mouth. After two long minutes of silence, Alex got his wish.

"Now is not the time to demand a pay rise."

"You said that yesterday. Why not today while business is good for us?"

"Because times are about to get very tough and I don't think the other syndicate members will appreciate a shakedown. Not now. Not anytime, really."

"You've known him way longer than me. How do we stop Albert?"

"Good question. I could try to have a quiet word with him and see if I can soften his position."

"Soften? If he goes to Charlie and the rest of the fellas, we'll be tarred with the same brush. All three of us will seem like gonifs."

"Alex, I might get him to reconsider his attitude, but it'll be a miracle if I could actually prevent him from demanding more money from the fellas."

"You think I should speak with Charlie and explain the situation before Albert makes a move?"

"If you do that and he finds out then he will never forgive you for going behind his back and dishonoring him."

"He blows hot and cold though, doesn't he? I don't know if it is his Italian blood or just that he's a *schmendrick.*"

"Never make the mistake of underestimating him, Alex. He blusters away most of the time, but he got to the top of his family by being a formidable leader. His temper might be his weakness, but it is also his towering strength."

He listened to Louis' words and took counsel. Anastasia had the potential to ruin the golden goose of Murder Corporation, but his desire to seize on an opportunity was one that Alex recognized in himself.

14

DUTCH SCHULTZ HAD built his empire off the back of bootlegging, like so many other members of the syndicate, but he had spread his wings considerably and included the numbers and union racketeering in his arsenal. Over the years, he had seen his fair share of trouble, especially when one of his own lieutenants had tried to take control of Dutch's domain through force.

Nobody was surprised when Vincent Coll, the Irish hitman in question, was gunned down in a telephone booth one February night three years earlier. Now Dutch had a problem and had asked Alex to visit him for a quiet word in his penthouse apartment at the Lexington Hotel, which Dutch kept for daytime business meetings and nighttime assignations.

The decor was pleasant enough inside this plush hotel but nothing of any note, thought Alex. The pattern of the wallpaper reminded him of Sarah's room in the Oregon, which, given the contrast in the two locations, raised a smile in the corner of Alex's mouth.

"Something amuse you, Alex?"

"Nope, just reminiscing, Dutch. This room reminds me of a place I used to visit."

"Try to keep your attention on our current troubles, if you don't mind."

Alex listened as Dutch explained how Shea Coll, Vincent's half-brother, had appeared in town two nights before, asking for Dutch's whereabouts.

"I don't bear the guy any ill will, but I am concerned he might have turned up in the city intending to do me harm."

"That sounds like a genuine concern given the bad blood between you and Vincent."

"And this brings me to why I wanted us to have a discreet conversation. While I am thrilled to deal with this matter myself, I don't want this to get out of hand. Where there is one half sibling, there could be more waiting to come out of the woodwork like roaches."

"Are you in need of an exterminator?"

"I can kill my own insects, thank you, but I want everyone to see that this is not some stupid vendetta. If you are with me on this, people will conclude this Coll got whacked because of some syndicate business."

"As I understand the situation, this is not a syndicate hit, though, is it?"

"Oh no. This is a private contract between the two of us and nobody else must know about the arrangement."

"I can certainly remove this man permanently and his mortal remains will never be found."

"Alex, you need not go to that much trouble. All I want you to do is to accompany me on the hit so that if anyone recognizes us, then they'll see it is not just me with a piece and a hot head."

Alex smiled for the second time in their conversation—Dutch was a tremendous syndicate member who generated considerable income for all with whom he worked, but he was famed for his uneven temper. He and Albert had much in common.

THERE COMES A point in every man's life that he draws heavily on the third cigarette in a row, stood outside a theater, watching a news booth on the other side of the street. Dutch had been given a tipoff from one of his guys that Shea was staying in a nearby fleapit and was in the habit of walking down this drag in the early evening before crashing out in his crib for the rest of the night. Mostly he was alone, but occasionally there was a moll with him.

Alex received Dutch's elbow in his ribs just as he spotted the same guy in a black trench coat with a brunette on his arm. Alex threw his smoke onto the ground and squished it with his foot. Shea bought the late edition from the booth and walked his skirt a block east, all the while shadowed by Alex and Dutch, one on each side of the street.

Shea turned right and Alex found himself within feet of the guy as he shuffled along with his girl in tow. The guy didn't notice him and carried on along the sidewalk as if Alex weren't there. Another block and Shea crossed over and Alex let Dutch take the lead as he was now nearer the guy.

Instead, Alex trailed the three blocks until Shea came to a halt outside a tenement building, no more interesting than any other nearby. Dutch kept on walking past the couple as they talked and Alex watched as Shea leaned into the girl, who giggled a few times and allowed the man to flirt with her a while on her stoop.

As they stood rooted to the same spot for over five minutes, Alex did his best to blend into the night and he propped himself up against the wall of a building near the junction, smoking a cigarette and pretending that this looked normal. Luckily, Dutch circled back and caught up with Alex a minute later.

"Any idea what we'll do next, Alex?"

"We could run across the street, all guns blazing and blast a cap in each of them."

"Okay, are you packing enough heat?"

"I was joking, Dutch. There are easier ways to deal with Coll than waking up the neighborhood."

Dutch looked at him quizzically, as if to show that Alex's suggestion was perfectly fine as far as he was concerned and there was no need to confuse matters with humor.

"The biggest issue is what will happen with that broad, Dutch."

"I don't mind if we whack her too."

"That may well be so, but I care. In our line of work, we try not to hit civilians and if possible, we avoid calling attention to ourselves. If

Coll goes up to the skirt's apartment then we should wait for another time when he is alone."

"Alex, I want this situation dispensed with tonight and that is the end of the matter. This is not a discussion."

As if to emphasize Dutch's point, as soon as he finished uttering his words, the couple entered the building. Alex thought for a spell, trying to figure out how they would even find Shea now he was hidden inside the tenement.

"You know which is her nest, Dutch?"

"Not a clue."

"Looks like we've got a problem on our hands then."

Coincidence abounded because that was when a light popped on in a third-floor apartment on the right-hand corner as the two men aimlessly stared at the building.

"Must have been them, right?"

Alex nodded and threw the remains of his cigarette on the ground.

"At least we have a location, although I haven't figured out how we can eliminate him without taking out the skirt."

"Alex, that's your problem, not mine—provided Coll is dead before dawn, I don't give a damn how many women you kill."

This was no longer a simple hit and Dutch's desire to get the job done this evening ran counter to all that Alex thought was sensible, but Dutch was paying for the contract and he had agreed to the deal. There was no backing out of it now. Alex sighed, put his hands in his pants pockets and sidled across the street, just as Shea appeared out of the entrance and hurtled past him with no flicker of recognition or acknowledgement that he had nearly knocked Alex over in his rush to leave the building.

Alex glanced up and the corner light remained on—looked like Coll had been sent out on an errand because the dame was staying put. Or he'd been thrown out on his ass and was heading home. Either way, Alex counted to ten and followed Shea at a respectful distance, leaving Dutch to stare at the glow of the apartment.

His route zigzagged from one corner to the next, all the while his path across town formed a large figure of eight. Fifteen minutes of what appeared to be mindless wandering later and Shea reached a small diner, the first place open since he'd left the tenement. You'd have thought it'd be easier to find a food joint in this city.

Shea went inside and Alex hustled to a position where he could see what was going on without standing immediately in front. There was a takeout counter and an old couple who occupied one of the three tables. The guy who must have been the owner stood behind the bar and appeared to be counting the day's takings.

A handful of muffled words and the boss beckoned toward the back of the joint and Shea tipped his hat and strode to the phone booth. An all-too-brief call later and he returned to the counter and bought some smokes. Alex decided now was the time to act.

He pushed through the door, eyed the seated couple who were too busy ignoring each other behind raised newspapers to give him any attention, and stepped toward Shea. The owner took one look at Alex, knew there was trouble ahead and ducked down, still clutching the notes from the day's earnings.

Alex whipped out his pistol and with a straight arm, fired two shots into Shea—one in the heart and the other to his head. The couple dropped their papers, glanced at each other and, with no comment or fuss, slipped out of the front and vanished into the night. They were so fast that they almost bumped into Alex on his way through the door.

Nobody stopped him or halted his progress along the deserted sidewalk. The sound of the gunfire must have been heard by some locals, but no sirens appeared and no cops had been called. Alex bet on the fact that the owner would plead ignorance when the flatfeet eventually came calling. If not, he was a dead man.

15

ATLANTIC CITY WAS the traditional home of meetings comprising the entire syndicate board. Once, it had taken place in the Catskills, but Charlie knew the fellas preferred a location where there was betting rather than borscht. There were more choices for female companionship in A.C. too.

The great and the good sat around an enormous boardroom table, each flanked by at least one of their lieutenants. Charlie, Meyer, Benny, Albert—the list was long and if you were responsible for any significant piece of criminal activity on the East Coast or parts of the Midwest, then you were in that hotel room, sipping your coffee or stroking the side of your water glass. As leader of the syndicate, Charlie began proceedings by tapping the back of a spoon on the side of his glass until there was silence.

"Thank you all for coming and taking time out of your busy schedules. As you know, we only meet when there is something significant to discuss or decide and today is one of those days."

Many nods and assenting murmurs from the assembled throng. Alex was impressed by how quickly these men had gathered together—Charlie had only issued the invitations on Friday and it was Monday now. They all understood how serious the situation would become.

"There are two issues we must agree on and they are intertwined. First, there is the question of what we shall do once the Volstead Act is repealed across the country. Second, we have benefitted from the fact that the Feds have been spread very thin across the land dealing with Prohibition violations. Soon, we won't have that luxury and we should expect them to come down on us hard—real hard."

Further murmuring ensued until Charlie called them to order. The number of people who had died as a result of the actions of the men in this room was countless and potentially unknown, but they still dutifully waited for each other to finish and even raised their hands to get attention and acknowledgement from the chair before they spoke. Sugar House gang leader Abe was the first to deal with their problems head on.

"Fellas, we are about to lose somewhere between a quarter and one half of our revenue and, Charlie is right, the cops will hit us with all their might. Doing nothing is not an option. In Detroit, we have already made plans—increasing our grip on the unions, edging other gangs not part of the syndicate out of town. But I can guarantee you that this will not be enough when the money from booze floats away."

"Joe Citizen won't want to go to our speakeasies," Meyer added. "An illegal drink was seen as a harmless pleasure, so our establishments were tolerated when the Federal government failed to give the people what they wanted. As soon as they can get a beer in a bar without any of us stood near them, they'll grab that opportunity with both hands. And no offense to anybody sat in this room. I am just giving my opinion of the average john."

Everyone knew that the syndicate's banker described their world perfectly and nobody was so foolish to believe that good citizens visited blind pigs because of the quality of the hooch or the owners of the joints. Cheap booze was all they cared about and they would go somewhere more comfortable and legal as soon as the opportunity arose.

Many of the syndicate members stood up to describe the problem of losing bootlegging from their perspectives, but there were no answers and no fresh ideas. Even though he didn't feel he had much to say, Alex didn't want to be left out from the roster—being seen to contribute on this stage might be useful to how these men viewed him. He changed topic so that his words would be more memorable. "Whatever we do, we need to address the issue of the cops."

"Let's hit them now before they have time to attack us," thundered Benny Siegel's voice above the noise of the general discussion. Trust Benny to take the direct approach, although no one was surprised because this was his usual carrion cry.

"We should stop talking and do it now." Dutch Schultz's response was less predictable and the rest of the group hushed to silence as Benny's suggestion received such vocal support.

"Benny, who do you think we should hit and how do you think it would help?"

Charlie looked at him with the corner of his mouth curled up, as though he was doing his best to show Benny respect, but he thought the idea was absurd. Alex knew this because he'd had a similar conversation with Charlie only four days ago.

"Hoover. Let's cut off the head of the snake."

"Benny, do you not think such an action might call attention to us? Are we not better to be more nuanced and perhaps look at ways of taking advantage of the inherent vulnerability of the flatfeet rather than hit the chief of the Bureau of Investigation?"

"If we act now, then they'll think twice about doing anything attacking us later."

This comment caused everybody in the room to express their views loudly and all at the same time. Charlie's attempt to quieten down the throng simply using a spoon and a glass was doomed to failure and he stopped trying within two seconds of starting.

AN HOUR LATER, everyone had calmed down and many had walked out to get away from the arguments taking place in the room. Nobody wanted to be the one to start any fight, but Benny and Dutch were both razor-thin close to getting their throats cut.

Alex kept himself calm by remaining near his crew—Ezra and Massimo were attending too, like many other lieutenants. With them being there, Alex let his attention wander briefly from the main stage to make sure their heads were in the right place.

"Dutch is an interesting guy."

"You can say that again, Ezra."

"Alex, you worked with him recently. Is he always like this?"

"Far be it from me to badmouth a member of the syndicate, but he is quick to reach conclusions—that's for certain, Massimo."

"Do you think we should kill Hoover?"

"No, Ezra. I had an opportunity to assassinate Eliot Ness, back in the day, and I let him live. No good comes from killing police officers. They are like cockroaches—as soon as you squash one, ten more appear out of the skirting and then a hundred more. Leave them alone and hope they'll pass you by—that's the best to expect."

"And if that doesn't work, bribe them?"

"Sure thing, Massimo, but keep your dignity. Those vermin will chew through your arm if you show them your hand."

BEFORE ANYONE COULD respond to Alex's dim view of law enforcement, Charlie called for everyone to sit down, which the attendees dutifully did. Those who were still outside were brought in by their lieutenants. Charlie stood up and the room fell silent with no clanging against any glass—the fire in his eyes spoke volumes.

"Gentlemen, we might not have consensus on how to handle inquisitive cops—although most of you agree with me—but this does not change the fact that we must shift out of bootlegging and into an altogether fresh line of business."

"Many of us have spent sleepless nights wrestling with this problem and we have only found one area ripe for exploitation."

"Meyer, explain to us your findings."

"We all know that we have a second-to-none transportation network and considerable storage facilities. To say we control vast swathes of retail space is also an understatement. The question is, what product can we fill it with?"

"Get on with it!" called out Benny, and Meyer scowled at his friend.

"What substance can we buy cheaply and sell for maximum profit that sits outside the law otherwise Rockefeller would have invested in it already?"

"Heroin," Charlie replied almost as if the speech had been rehearsed. "With my Sicilian connections, we could start shipping the opiate in a large scale into the country within a matter of weeks. We turn warehouses into laboratories to cut the stuff into street-grade heroin and then use our guys to sell it on the sidewalks."

"And the profit is so huge we'll ask ourselves why we ever bothered with booze," Meyer noted.

A million conversations broke out all at once, but Charlie let them happen—he and Meyer had lit a fire in everyone's belly and he didn't want it to go out. Ten minutes later, Alex could see that most debate had died down and Charlie took control of the room again.

"So we can all benefit from this opportunity, we need to get organized for the new business. And we must also make sure we keep an eye on all our existing activities. There's no point making money peddling heroin if we lose our regular payments from unions or protection money from local businesses."

Charlie nodded at Albert who was keen to speak.

"Some of us have concentrated our attention on other matters and are not best placed to take advantage of this new opportunity. How are we going to do this fairly, because whenever there's a vast amount of money being made, there are differences of opinion that Murder Corporation will have to tidy up? We won't have the time to build supply lines for heroin."

"That is what we are here to ensure, Albert. Every one of us should dip their beaks and benefit from the good fortune presented to us today. We will all contribute to the success of the heroin trade and we shall get paid a fair amount—once those who have expenses have those costs covered. After all, we are not communists."

A ripple of laughter and rueful smiles floated across the hotel room.

"Let's have a show of hands—who is in favor of moving into the heroin business?"

Nearly every arm was raised and Charlie announced the motion carried almost unanimously. Then he outlined his plan to bring in one shipment and to follow its progress from boat to Brownsville street corner. They would sell to their own for the time being and iron out all the wrinkles before expanding the operation.

They'd learned much in the early days of bootlegging and knew they would achieve more through a stealthy increase in production which the cops might not notice until they were completely set up. Then it would be too late. Alex was pleased Charlie had included him on the inside track those weeks before—he'd had no surprises today apart from Benny and Dutch's desire to attack law enforcement. Thoughts of heroin drew his mind to Ida for a second, but Massimo confronted him with more immediate issues.

"You going back tonight, Alex, or will you stay with us and party?"

JULY 1935

16

HEROIN FLOWED FROM Palermo through the Eastern Seaboard and onto the streets of New York, just as Charlie had promised. The profit margin was incredible and all syndicate members enjoyed the collective wealth generated from the brown powder.

As everybody got fatter on the tremendous opportunity that heroin dealing afforded, there was an inevitable heightening in tension between different parts of the organization. The leaders of Murder Corporation had earned their salaries since that syndicate meeting.

Now Albert, Louis and Alex sat for the umpteenth time in Albert's restaurant on Mulberry for another bowl of pasta and a discussion.

"We need to raise our rates."

No sooner had the words left Albert's lips than Alex's heart sank. Apart from greed, he saw no reason for the Italian to open this ancient conversation again. Hadn't this been resolved years ago?

"Do you not think we are making enough at the moment?"

"Alex, our outfit has always been almost pure profit because of what we do," interjected Louis, "But that doesn't mean we are being paid the appropriate rate by the syndicate."

"Sure, but equally it doesn't mean we are being underpaid either, does it?"

All three chewed on their food and mulled the issue over in their minds. Alex was the first to break cover.

"The price for killing a man has increased every year and payments are always made on time—within a day or two of the event occurring. With business booming and everything going as well as it is, I don't think we should seek any extra payments—at least not now. If the contracts dry up then by all means let's increase the amount we charge so we still end up with the same income. These suits don't grow on trees."

Alex flicked a bit of fluff off his sleeve to stress his point and brushed the wool material down where it had been momentarily shifted by his fingers. It was a beautiful piece of *schmatta*.

"Alex, forgive me—you are right. There are more important things for us to do than argue with Luciano over money."

"Absolutely. We should talk about the unions instead, at the very least."

Louis spoke as though Alex was meant to know what he was talking about, but he had no idea at all. Albert pounced on the silence created by this strange statement.

"You're right, Louis. While we have guys waiting for a call from Reles to make a hit, we could use their muscle for other activities."

"And that involves the unions?"

"Why not, Alex? There are many businesses in Midtown that are unionized but we have no influence either with the workers or their bosses. That's gelt we are leaving on the table."

"Have you been scouting around looking for easy pickings, Louis?"

"No, he hasn't, but I have instead."

"And what have you found, Albert?"

"There's not much opportunity downtown or even Midtown. Our outfits have worked this territory for thirty or more years by now, but if we go up to East Harlem, then there are many businesses whose workers need to be protected from the likes of us or require support from us to support their fight against the evil capitalist masters."

"Surely there are already gangs offering these services?"

"There are, Alex, but they are local and have yet to get affiliated with any syndicate member and that is where we can step in and help them."

Alex pondered Albert's words over two mouthfuls of linguini and wondered why the Italian would mention this now—and more interestingly, why was Louis so keen? Had they hatched a plan between them and were hoping to get a nod from Alex and then push him out before the game had even begun?

This made no sense as the two men could set themselves up to take over East Harlem territory without even mentioning it to Alex, because it was none of his business. However, Alex didn't want to come across as negative and chose his reply with the utmost care.

"I'm perfectly happy to get involved in some union bashing—I earned my spurs doing the same thing a lifetime ago under Waxey Gordon."

"Excellent news. We hoped that would be the case. Are you prepared to head north a few blocks and slam heads?"

"That I can do, but I assume we will all three need to encourage the locals to pay us for the right to carry on their daily duties."

"We thought that as you were so successful on the waterfront that you'd like to repeat that performance on dry land."

Alex swallowed hard as his heart sank at the implications of Albert's suggestion.

THE ENTHUSIASM SHOWN by Albert and Louis for Alex to get his hands dirty in the business of union racketeering was noticeable. He hoped it was only his imagination, but a gnawing doubt remained whispering in his ear like a weevil on his shoulder.

"We've all had experience hammering the unions, surely? Albert, I can't believe you got to where you are without cracking a few convener heads."

"That's not the point, Alex. The issue is, who of us is best placed to work on the ground in East Harlem. Louis and I have several other business interests beyond Murder Corporation and I don't believe you are so encumbered, right?"

"I have interests outside of our contracts. I might not talk about them, but they are there."

Louis eyed Albert and then cast his gaze over to Alex, whose spine was stiff with indignation. They were both treating him like their lieutenant and not their equal. He couldn't understand why they were behaving this way.

"I don't want to get into any chest-beating competition with you, but our activities are considerable—I'm sure you'll agree, Alex."

"No contest, Albert, but that is not my point. As we all three are busy men, if we wanted to, we could get some of our fellas to the donkeywork."

Alex stared at Louis, wondering why he was allowing Albert to behave this way—or perhaps the situation was reversed. Albert had influenced or instructed Louis to follow his lead—there was more gelt for Louis with Anastasia than with this Cohen.

Then Alex's thoughts turned to a darker place and he considered the possibility that the reason they wanted him on the street was that would increase his chances of getting attacked or killed. Why else were they so eager for him to take personal charge of a campaign that Ezra, Massimo, or a whole host of guys could run? Not for the first time during this meeting, he swallowed hard. Was this the beginning of the end?

17

THE MEETING ENDED with no real conclusion. Alex's intransigence prevented him from committing to take to the streets and strong-arm union officials and Albert was too hungry with the desire to seize territory and screw down the unions even further. In the end, they agreed to work together, which in practice meant Albert would encourage Louis to use his men instead of Alex. Meantime, Charlie and Meyer kept Alex close as they dealt with information gleaned from Lansky's informers.

"We said it would happen and we were not wrong."

"What are you talking about, Meyer?"

"A special prosecutor has been named, whose job it is to hit organized crime, Alex."

"We're disorganized most of the time so we've got nothing to worry about, right?"

"I wish. Thomas Dewey's been told to root out extortion, prostitution, and racketeering. He'll have us squarely in his sights."

"Are you really worried, Charlie?"

"Better believe it. This guy has a reputation for being cleaner than clean and Mayor Lehman will hand him more than sixty of New York City's finest to help him make arrests and get convictions. This is serious."

"And only four months ago, Hoover renamed his flatfeet to the Federal Bureau. The men in suits are getting mighty feisty."

Alex contemplated Meyer's words.

"Surely if we grease the right palms, they'll find someone else to pick on."

"Perhaps, Alex. I mean, if we can. From what I've heard from our inside contact, these guys are squeaky upright."

"Yes, Meyer, but the office cleaners, the stenographers, the girls in the typing pool—they are much more easily bought. And for less money."

Alex smiled at Charlie's comment but couldn't help wondering if they would survive until fall. With Anastasia nipping at his heels and potentially Dewey biting at their ankles, what chance did he have for a peaceful few months?

WITHIN A WEEK of Dewey's task force getting an office, the special prosecutor sent his men out to hit the streets—and attack every operation they could find. Any fella who ran a significant angle in New York was on the receiving end of a visit from the gumshoes and their baseball bats. If they had been crooks, then heads would have been cracked.

As it was, doors were smashed, nefarious property bagged and removed. Worst of all, no one put their hand out to be taken care of— every man jack of them was on the up and up. One of Albert's guys tried to offer a Dewey officer a small token of his appreciation to leave the premises and was promptly arrested. Nobody could remember times quite like this.

"What are we going to do about this special prosecutor?"

"Charlie, are you saying you want me to whack Dewey?"

"Alex, that couldn't be further from my thoughts. Please don't even joke about such matters."

Meyer, Charlie, Benny, and Alex sat in the usual booth at the back of Lindy's. Four coffees and three slices of cake were on the table in front of them—Benny wasn't hungry.

"What are we going to do about this menace then, Charlie?"

"That is a question in desperate need of an answer."

Benny chuckled for far too long—so much so that Meyer glared at him to stop. For Alex, the problem of Dewey was already hitting his bank balance.

"Contracts have reduced with the Corporation."

"The crackdowns are making everyone cautious—so there is less friction between fellas as their activities are slowing down."

"Right, Meyer."

Benny laughed again and wouldn't stop.

"What is so goddamn funny?"

"Alex, can't you see that he's doing his job even when Dewey's not breaking down our doors? By attacking a handful of us and making a big deal about it, the cop's reach is far bigger than the fifty chumps he's put on the street."

"That's not funny—it is pitiful and that is costing us gelt, Benny."

"I know, Meyer, but you have to laugh otherwise you cry."

"I am not amused."

"Charlie, no disrespect but I am not changing who I am."

"I understand, Benny. I am not asking you to change, but to remain silent and not distract us as we wrestle with this problem. If this carries on then by the end of the year, you will have less money in your wallet and then you'll be laughing on the other side of your face, *boychik*."

Benny raised his eyebrows high because he couldn't remember the last time he had heard Charlie Luciano use Yiddish. This really was serious and they all fell silent, eating cake and occasionally slurping their coffees. Charlie broke the spell.

"For now, all we can do is tread carefully and not give Dewey any excuses to arrest any of us. Just because he's hitting warehouses today doesn't mean he won't look at our record keeping tomorrow."

"You think he'll copy Ness and hit our tax filings?"

"Why not? If they can take down Alfonse with a pile of paper, do you believe we are any more safe, Alex?"

"I have always ensured I operate through a legitimate company and have a trail of invoices to justify some of my income."

"You're a shrewd cookie, Meyer. I don't have a single document to my name. All the details are in my head."

"Alex, I've got oodles of sales and purchase dockets. You have some of mine if you like."

"Thanks, Charlie. I might take you up on that offer."

"You're welcome. Now, back to business. Until we can get some concrete information from our rat in Dewey's offices, we must also be very careful what we say and who we say it in front of. Loose talk will cost us our lives."

JERVIS MCCRACKEN SAUNTERED into Lindy's restaurant two days later and sat in the rearmost booth, much to the distress of the waitering staff. He only had to wait ten minutes before Charlie walked in and headed to his usual location, followed by Alex thirty seconds afterward. They both stopped in their tracks when they saw McCracken at their table.

"You seem to have been given the wrong table, Mac."

"I'm at the right place—and my name's not Mac."

Charlie sat down opposite the guy and twirled a match around his thumb and first finger, never taking his eyes off the stranger in front of him. Alex perched next to Charlie because he had no desire to be on the same side of the table as this unknown operator to get stabbed if the fella unleashed a temper.

"What do you want, little man?"

"I'm here to give you a piece of friendly advice and I hope you listen well to what I have to say."

"Go on."

Alex remained *schtum* and left Charlie to do all the talking. Just as Jervis was about to respond, Meyer arrived, five minutes late for their meeting. He looked at the situation, swallowed and caught Alex's eye, turned tail, and promptly exited the building.

"You and your people have two options and we really don't mind which one you choose. You can cease your criminal activities with immediate effect or we will come after you and take you down."

"Thanks for sharing your opinions. Who do you think you are exactly and why should I pay any attention to some shriveling lump of nothing who sits in restaurants and tries to threaten men before they even order a coffee…?"

"…and a piece of cake."

McCracken looked at Alex and back at Charlie—then he laughed.

"I work for Thomas Dewey. You will have heard of him because he has made it his sworn duty to convict every single last pond scum like you two breathing in New York City."

Charlie cracked his knuckles and smiled at Alex, who smirked back. He leaned forward a few inches, encouraging Jervis to mirror his body language. He stared at the cop, holding his gaze for five, ten seconds. When he spoke, his voice was barely a whisper.

"Now you listen to me and you listen real careful. Nobody comes to my restaurant and threatens me, you capiche? We told you before, we are here for some light refreshments and yet you accuse us with nothing to back you up. No evidence, no proof, and no bodyguard. That makes you a very foolish man. The next time you loudly attack me for being a criminal, you'd better have more to show for yourself than an ill-fitting suit and a sanctimonious grin on your face, you odious string of piss."

The corners of McCracken's mouth dropped and he gulped. Maybe he wasn't used to being spoken to with such disrespect—perhaps he felt the fear that ordinary men experienced in the presence of Charlie Luciano.

"Now it is your turn to listen to me. I came here in the spirit of friendship to let you know that you have a choice and that you do not have to end up behind bars. If you turf me out of this establishment, then you will have made your decision. And that is fine with me, because what we want is to rid this town of crime—we don't care how, just so long as it happens. The next time I come in here, I'll have a warrant in my hand or a subpoena in my pocket. Either way, you'll be walking out in handcuffs."

Jervis popped his hat on his head, thrust his hands in his pants pockets and waltzed out of Lindy's, whistling a tune, never looking back.

◆ ◆ ◆

THE NEXT DAY, hell descended on the streets of the five boroughs. Dewey's men hit at least one significant operation of every member of the syndicate who was based in New York—almost as if they had mapped out the entire criminal fraternity in the city. Over the following two weeks, it felt as if each cathouse, gaming den and heroin facility had been raided.

Alex's transportation network was in tatters—many of his vehicles had been confiscated, pending proof they had been used in criminal activities. He wasn't too worried because most trucks were not actually owned by him in the first place so most of the mud would not stick.

Other syndicate members were not as relaxed about the situation. Meanwhile, others took advantage of the attention given by the cops to the Big Apple and focused their aim on other places like Boston. So Alex was not surprised when he received a call, and grabbed a train to carry out a contract for Murder Corporation.

18

FRANK MORELLI HAD made the request to the syndicate for a hit on Charles Solomon's son. The youth had been snapping at his heels ever since Frank assassinated the boy's father two years before. Then he didn't waste time seeking permission and asked for forgiveness after he'd consolidated his power base from his North End headquarters in Boston.

On this occasion, Alex held a contract on Hayim because Frank couldn't be bothered to carry out his own dirty work. The boy—twenty years old—was more a thorn in Frank's side than anything else and the boss of Boston could wait an extra day to rid himself of this nuisance with the minimum of fuss.

Whenever Alex spent time in Puritan City, he noticed how calm the place felt compared to New York. There was still a hustle and bustle as people made their way about their daily tasks, but the edge was missing—that feeling you always had to be on your toes when you walked the Midtown streets.

A cab ride from South Station on Summer Street to Charter Street took no time at all, and soon Alex sat opposite Frank to discuss the reason for his journey.

"There is a boy who has made threats, spouted big talk to his friends in public and generally showed me disrespect."

"Frank, you need not justify the hit to me—the syndicate has authorized it and here I am."

"Sure, Alex, but I knew him when he was growing up—I held him in my arms as a newborn."

"Sometimes they fail to come out of the oven properly."

"And you don't think it has anything to do with the fact I had his papa whacked?"

"Occasionally, Frank, the bread gets misshapen when it is dropped on the floor and trodden on."

They both smiled because Alex was correct on both counts. Why Hayim was in this situation was entirely because of his father's hit and the fact he complained about it rather than take matters into his own hands. Now the syndicate had sanctioned the killing, Frank's justifications were in the past—Hayim Solomon had to die and it was Alex's job to see that it happened before his return to New York.

"What information can you give me about the kid's whereabouts?"

"There are a number of cafés where he goes during the day when he's not making his collections. And in the evenings there are a thousand dives he drinks and cavorts in."

"Is he always with his crew during his daytime exploits?"

"Yeah, I mean apart from one or two visits he makes to special clients, but in the evening he's hanging around with the kids in his neighborhood. They go to all different joints—whichever place is in fashion that night. The Cotton Club was good enough back in my day, but the world has changed."

Alex nodded, although he hadn't gone to a nightclub to dance ever since he started owning them. He guessed Frank was cut from the same cloth.

"Let me watch his movements and then I can decide the best course of action. From now on, I will only contact you if there is something specific I need. I'll drop a dime before I leave town so you know it is done. Apart from that, is there anybody you could lend me while I am here?"

"For the job or for evening companionship?"

"The hit. I don't mix business with pleasure."

"And here was me thinking you find eternal happiness in your work."

"It has its moments, but no skirt to recognize me in a line-up, thanks all the same."

Both men shared a laugh, shook hands and Frank introduced Alex to Savio Altimari—tall, thin, eyes that would shoot bullets given half a moment.

ALEX ASKED SAVIO to walk the streets with him—it gave the out-of-towner an opportunity to get to know North End a little and to pick the local's brain.

"You worked with Frank long?"

"Long enough."

"How well would you say you know Junior?"

"Who?"

"Hayim Solomon."

"Oh, since before his father met with an untimely end."

"What do you make of him?"

"The guy has a chip on his shoulder and who can blame him? If I were him though, I'd have kept my mouth shut and done something about it instead."

"Really? That'd be what you'd have done?"

"Well, if I'd been the son of a gang boss, I'd have done it."

Alex smiled at Silvio, who showed tremendous understanding of the hierarchy in play in their world. The lieutenants did the bidding of their bosses and the bosses behaved however they wanted.

"So where's the best place to find Hayim right now?"

"He'll be looking after his special clients along Snow Hill Street."

"What makes them special? Frank described them like that too."

"Let's head over there and you can see for yourself."

WHEN THEY ARRIVED, Alex saw the usual mix of stores, apartment blocks and a variety of people on the sidewalks. Nothing and nobody appeared that unusual, but he minded himself and waited with Silvio, as they leaned against a wall and lit a cigarette each.

Ten minutes later, Silvio nudged Alex as a young man sauntered along the sidewalk on the opposite side of the street, heading left. At the third entrance, Hayim stopped, put a hand on the door handle, looked both ways up and down the street, and entered the building.

"What gives?"

"One of his specials."

"Looks like any other apartment block to me."

"It does, doesn't it?" Silvio said with a wry smile on his face.

Thirty long minutes and Hayim reappeared, adjusted his jacket, and carried on in the same direction as before. Two blocks later and the same thing happened—into a nondescript building, remained for more minutes than any human might need to collect a wad of gelt and then back out onto the street. After the third time, one block farther on, Alex was tired of watching and waiting.

"Am I going to follow the kid in to find out what's occurring or will you just tell me?"

"No mystery. These are cathouses and Hayim likes to taste the product when he picks up the day's takings. There are four more joints further down this street and two more around the corner. Hayim'll be busy for the rest of the afternoon."

Alex nodded and conjured with the viable ways he could attack Hayim on his route, but either he'd be highly visible on a sidewalk or he would be seen in one of the bordellos. Neither option sounded great.

"If you like, Alex, we could go for a bowl of pasta and meet up with the kid in two hours' time. I know the location of his last port of call. That way, we can rest our shoe leather."

THEIR TABLE WAS at the rear of the Italian restaurant which Silvio took them to and, judging by his reception when they arrived, the owners knew him well. Alex ensured he kept his fedora down over his eyes until they were ensconced at the back. Even then, he made sure he sat in the shadows, not wanting anybody to identify him as being in Boston should the unfortunate occasion arise.

"Relax, you are safe here. Nobody knows anyone or sees anything in this place."

"How can you be so certain?"

"Frank owns the joint. If anyone blabs, then they'll float in the Charles River by dusk."

With those words, Alex relaxed and ordered linguini with salmon and a coffee. Once the food had been delivered and the waiter had walked out of earshot, their conversation continued.

"What about the evenings? Frank said how Hayim never visited the same joint twice."

"Not quite. He is right that every few days there's a new venue for the kids to be seen in, but there are two points where you can guarantee you know the whereabouts of our hero."

"And?"

"Hayim returns to his crib to change into his nightclub threads—around six or so, depending on how busy he's been on Snow Hill Street. The creature of habit returns to his own bed at night. If there's a skirt with him then he never goes to her place, always brings her back to his lair. And usually throws her out onto the street by the early hours. It would appear our boy likes to sleep alone."

Alex smiled at the possibilities this news offered and checked his watch—four twenty. He could polish off the linguini, whack the guy and still make it back home tonight.

SILVIO TOOK ALEX over to Hayim's apartment block and gave him the door number. Then he shook hands and walked away–a job well done. Alex moved round the rear of the building and shimmied up the fire escape three floors and jimmied open the sash window with a knife he carried for this purpose. He scooted inside and ensured the frame was completely closed again, before checking out the place.

It was a simple affair—bedroom, bathroom, living room and kitchen all leading off from the hallway. Nothing fancy and the kind of accommodation suitable for a single man in his twenties. Another look at his watch and Alex reckoned the guy should appear some time in the next forty minutes.

Alex positioned himself behind the living room door. From this vantage point, he could see through the crack near the hinge, into the hallway and the apartment entrance. He leaned against the wall, knowing this was about to be the difficult, tedious phase of any campaign. Five minutes later his boredom was cut short as he heard a key being pushed into the lock and there stood Hayim, fiddling to remove the key. Alex held his breath and waited.

Finally, the boy wrestled the metal free and closed the door, heading straight for the bathroom. He swung the door to, but it didn't shut completely. The sound of liquid landing in the toilet bowl meant Alex understood exactly what to do next.

He ran through the hallway and kicked the door open so he'd have both hands free. Hayim turned round, but he was too late. Alex seized the back of his neck and pushed him sideways so his head slammed into the side of the shower. Crunch. Blood dribbled out of his skull and Hayim screamed.

Alex's spare palm covered the kid's mouth and he smashed Hayim's head twice into the ceramic floor of the shower unit. Muffled yelps, but the boy got his bearings and struggled to get out of Alex's clutches. With one hand round the back of Hayim's neck and the other still clasped over his mouth, Alex yanked him up and dragged him toward the sink.

A sharp motion forwards and Hayim's head smacked into the faucets. Once, twice, three times. Blood was streaming out of his mouth, an eye, and his forehead, and yet he wouldn't die. As much as Alex wanted this to be a silent kill, sometimes matters can get out of hand and this ox didn't want to lie down and die. So he pulled out his pistol, threw him with both hands into the back of the shower and shot him in the heart. Hayim slumped down, one leg twitching for fifteen seconds and then nothing.

Alex checked himself in the mirror above the sink and cleaned off Hayim's blood from his face and fingers. Luckily, there was no red on his clothes. He listened by the front door in case anyone was on the stairway, but nothing. Alex exited the building and walked four blocks before hailing a cab and asking to go to Beacon's Hill. From there he strolled two blocks and hailed a second taxi to take him to the station. Before he boarded his train, Alex popped into a phone booth and dropped a dime to Frank, as promised.

19

"HOW'S TRICKS?"

Charlie and Alex were spending an evening together in the back of one of Charlie's gaming joints, near Mulberry and Canal.

"Been better, but I won't complain."

"You never do, Charlie."

"I make more than enough money to keep me in clover. Why should I grouse when I can still afford three square meals and a roof over my head? You only have to look at the chumps on the street for a minute to know you're doing better than every single one of them."

"Murder Corporation revenue is down on last year, but we too are sitting pretty."

"Is that why Albert has been pushing into East Harlem without permission?"

"He's a made man and does what he thinks best."

"You didn't answer my question, Alex."

"You're right—and I'm not going to respond to it now. We both know that Louis and I can do nothing if Albert mops up some territory going spare. He doesn't need our permission to harangue Italian gangs on the up-and-up."

"Enough said. You heard from Benny recently?"

"Nah, he's a loner. Pops out from under his rock to break occasional bread with us, laugh at what we say, then go back into the soil. I like the guy, but he is strange."

"And no mistake. He and Meyer go way back. Besides, the guy knows how to handle himself and has a creative imagination. Sometimes that turns into little gold mines. You heard about Dutch?"

"Only what I read in the papers. Dewey is after him."

"And some. That cop has a hard-on for our boy."

"Anything we can do to help him?"

"He's got himself a lawyer—a good one—but the fella is a hothead and that means he's shot his mouth off in public one too many times. There are several witnesses, from what I hear, that tie Dutch's paperwork to income he hasn't declared or got a reason why."

"Tax evasion, Charlie, look what it did to Alfonse and see what it will do to Dutch."

"Tell me about it, Alex. It's funny because years ago we talked about the same subject and Meyer convinced me to run a legitimate shell company and now I feel a lot more secure. Having Meyer as my accountant helps too, of course. You?"

"Still no paperwork, no shell, bupkis."

"Alex, while Dewey is in New York, you'd better get yourself something to justify your income—otherwise you're on a one-way ticket to Sing Sing."

Alex stared coldly at Charlie because he knew his friend was right. Dewey would not go away just by ignoring him. He made a mental note to speak to Meyer and get some advice from the syndicate's consigliere.

THREE WEEKS LATER and Dutch's trial began. A stream of witnesses spoke of how the fella had not been where he said he was at the time when his paperwork showed he was out working at his clerical job. Then the IRS representatives walked the jury through all the details of each line of every invoice. Dewey ensured that the twelve good men and true could join the dots between the false claims made by the accused and the reality of what Dutch owned and earned.

Naturally, none of his allies could attend court and show any direct support, but in the evenings they'd meet up with him and discuss the day's events.

"I'm no Capone."

"You certainly kept a lower profile than Alfonse, but that doesn't mean you will walk away from this beef."

"Don't talk like that, Meyer. They aren't going to put me behind bars."

"I admire your spunk, Dutch, but if the newspaper reports are anything to go by, the evidence is building against you. It doesn't matter what those of us here believe—it is the jury that counts."

"Alex, that's easy for you to say as I'm the one looking at hard time."

"I'm only pointing out that you might want to think about how to give yourself an edge, Dutch."

Charlie smiled and Meyer tilted his head at Alex, deep in thought.

"What are you suggesting?"

"Have you considered an indirect route to a not guilty verdict if your lawyer can't get it for you the usual way?"

"You're talking like you got an idea, Alex."

"I was wondering what would happen if we could change the opinion of a juror—or two."

Dutch swallowed hard and considered Alex's proposal.

THE BEDROCK OF the American judicial system is that any man accused of a crime will be listened to by twelve of his equals. The prosecution and defense attorneys do their best to present evidence and argument to sway the opinion of the members of the jury, but the simple truth is this: what goes on inside the jury room, stays in the jury room and no one knows but those twelve.

And that was what Alex was banking on because he understood that the entire process operated on the basis that everyone is essentially good, whereas all the people he had ever met in his life demonstrated to him that every single person on this planet has a price and the trick is to find out what that amount is and offer just a little more to sweeten the deal further.

Alex sent Ezra out to the courthouse on the second day of the proceedings to check out the lay of the land. That night, he reported back.

"There are three potential John Does we could impress. One is rich —quality suits, the way he speaks. Number two is an obvious mark —he has turned up in the same shirt both days and would do anything for a buck."

"And the third?"

"He is quiet, doesn't mix with the other jurors. Any time someone talks, he scribbles away in a little notebook—takes himself seriously."

"That's the one we want. Follow him tomorrow and find out where we can bump into him on the way home."

"YOU GOT A light, Mac?"

"Sure. Here you go."

Alex thanked Matt Knowles and inhaled on his cigarette for a moment. The man smiled briefly and tried to push on down the street—he was only a block away from the bar where he consumed a single beer before going home. Alex blocked his route by leaning to one side—only a knowing eye would have spotted the move.

"I don't suppose you know a comfortable drinking place nearby?"

"Why, yes. As it happens, I'm heading that way myself."

"Mind the company?"

"Not at all."

There was a momentary hesitation which betrayed Knowles' instinct to be alone, but he had little choice, given Alex's friendly and innocent tone.

When they arrived at the tavern, Alex followed Matt to the bar and bought them both a beer. Matt thanked him for his generosity and turned to sit at what Alex knew to be his usual seat based on what Ezra had said.

Alex took a few sips of his drink from where he stood and then headed in Knowles' direction, much to his surprise.

"Mind if I share the table?"

"Well, I..."

Before Matt could express his actual opinion, Alex sat down and spread himself out opposite the hapless juror.

"What do you do for a living?"

"I'm an accounts clerk but I doubt I'll see the inside of my office for a while."

"Oh?"

"Yes, I am otherwise occupied at the moment."

"Doing what?"

Alex sipped his beer, indicating only a sociable interest in the response.

"I shouldn't say—we're not meant to talk about it."

"You a spy?"

"No, I'm on a jury—started this week."

"Juicy case?"

"Interesting enough. It's tax evasion."

"That doesn't sound too exciting. Anyone I've heard of?"

"Some Jew gangster, Dutch Flegenheimer."

Alex let the conversation twist around Schultz's situation until he took Matt's attention away from the unusual position of sharing a drink with a stranger who'd asked for a match.

"You think he's guilty?"

"What? I can't talk about the case—they were very clear about that."

"Sure, but you reckon he did it?"

Matt's eyes shifted right, then left. He shuffled on his chair and leaned in toward Alex as all conspirators do.

"There's no smoke without fire and you know what those people are like, right?"

"Are you certain? I mean, the trial's only been running two days. The defense might have something up their sleeve."

"Like stolen money?"

Knowles laughed at his own joke, but Alex stared straight at him without a glimmer of a smile.

"Let's not make light of a thing as important as this. The guy will be sent away for a long time if he's found guilty."

"And what if he was? Why do you care?"

"You like your apartment?"

"What? Sure. It's small, but I can afford the rent."

"Would you want to have a bigger place?"

"Sure, who wouldn't?"

"I could help you with that, if you'd like."

Matt put his beer down on the table and now it was his turn to look as serious as a heart attack at Alex.

"What d'you mean?"

"I have some friends who would show their appreciation if Dutch Schultz walks free."

"Friends?"

"Yep, and if that happened then you could afford a new apartment —with more space."

"I really don't think…"

"…and the other advantage of helping my associates is that you'd be alive to enjoy your new crib."

Matt stared at Alex and gulped.

"How can you be sure I won't go straight to the cops and turn you in?"

"I don't know that for sure, but there is one thing of which I am absolutely certain—if between now and the end of the trial, you visit a precinct station or talk to a cop about anything apart from to get directions then I guarantee you'll be dead before sunset. And then you'd need to think about how you would go about protecting your daughter—from your first marriage…"

Alex picked up his beer and downed what remained of the brew. He wiped his lips on the sleeve of his jacket and looked back at Matt, who had acquired tiny beads of sweat dripping off his cheeks and onto the table.

"Do we have an understanding?"

Matt Knowles nodded and Alex tipped his hat and walked out of the bar. They never met again, but on the day after the trial, Knowles discovered a brown paper bag in his mailbox that contained enough gelt to keep him in clover—and silent—for the rest of his days.

OCTOBER 1935

20

DESPITE ALL HIS fine words about ridding himself of the failed Yiddish actress, Ida Grynberg, Alex had done nothing about acting on those syllables for over five years. There were many months when he hardly visited her at all and later, whenever the mood descended on him, he would spend a week or two in her company before returning to his own suite and bed.

Ida never appeared to mind about his absences, wrapped as she was in her own theatrical world. When he turned up, she smiled and let him in and if he didn't show again, she carried on as though he was not in her life.

Following Alex's conversation with Knowles, he wanted to change his routine and spend a night with Ida. It wasn't the lure of sex, which was lackluster after all these years, but the desire for companionship, no matter how shallow that might be between them.

When he rang the doorbell, Alex had to wait an eternity for Ida to haul ass and open up for him. He had called before he left so he would be certain she was in and to give her a chance to get rid of any other guest, should any be in attendance. Alex didn't judge what she did when they weren't together—he had no high moral ground in this respect either.

When she eventually let him in, she smiled at him and pecked Alex on the cheek before twirling around and heading back to the apartment living room where she flopped onto the chaise longue.

"So glad to see you after all this time, Alex, darling."

"It has been a while—how are you doing, Ida. All well?"

"I have been absolutely divine, thank you for asking. How has the world of extortion and racketeering been to you?"

"No need to be like that, Ida. Business has been good, which is one reason it's been such a long time since we've been together. I'm hoping you'll be okay with me spending a few days with you now."

"Darling, that is absolutely priceless news."

ALEX WOKE UP next to Ida and did a double-take because he forgot where he was for a second. Then he shook off the sleep in his head and focused on his whereabouts until he recognized his location. Then he sighed inside when he recalled who he was with and why he was in Ida's bed.

He remained where he lay and enjoyed the silence of the early morning until his companion stirred ten minutes later. Alex had spent at least half that time staring at her naked back, trying to decide how much he still yearned for her physically. His conclusion was simple: while she wasn't unattractive, there was not enough about her to make him desire her anymore.

Not for the first occasion, Alex considered finding a fresh squeeze —one he might want to spend time with—but he knew himself sufficiently well to be aware that he wasn't really prepared to put in the required effort to sustain a relationship. If he was going to do that, then he would spend his energy trying to get Sarah back. And that had not happened since she walked out.

Ida stirred and rolled over to face him. She smiled and touched his chest briefly. Then she returned her arm under the covers to keep it warm.

"Good morning, darling. Be a love and light me a cigarette."

Alex nodded and hopped out of bed long enough to grab a packet of smokes and to rummage around until he found a book of matches. He lit two cigarettes and passed one to Ida. Then they lay next to each other, soaking in the warmth of each other's bodies. He wanted to find some kind of conversation with her, but no ideas sprang to mind until…

"Have you been in any productions recently?"

"Me, dear? No. There hasn't been a sniff of work for months. Sometimes I wonder if directors look at me and think I am too old for the lead roles."

"Really? I might not know much about the theater but how could anyone say you are mature?"

"You are sweet, but acting is a young girls' game. Nobody in the audience will look at me on stage and believe I could end up as a blushing bride when the curtain goes down."

"I still think it's crazy talk. Besides, you're a singer too."

"That I am, although my voice has seen better days. Too much smoking and living the high life have put paid to my vocal chords."

Alex found that hard to argue against—from the moment he saw her in the Richardson speakeasy, a blind pig he'd owned and run at the start of Prohibition, Ida's career had been going downhill and this period between roles was just the latest in a long line of tales she had offered him over the years.

AFTER THEY'D LAZED around for quite some time, Alex threw on his clothes while Ida sauntered to the kitchen and attended to their breakfast. She remembered he preferred a cup of strong coffee and maybe a slice of lightly buttered toast, but not much else.

Her idea of the opening meal of the day was a cigarette, so it didn't take her long to prepare the repast. Alex appreciated that she was trying as he tucked into the burned bread lying stiffly on his plate. At times like this, he wished he liked cereal—pouring milk on top of some flakes was less prone to culinary error.

They sat at the circular kitchen table, which stood by a window, to soak in as much of the natural light as possible. As he glanced at Ida, bathed in the sun's glow, Alex saw how haggard she appeared—the seasons had not been kind to her. She looked at least thirty years older than him, but he knew there were only ten separating them—

he had been a late teenager when she was in her twenties. Now you would never believe that to be the case.

Once he'd swallowed the last vestige of toast and washed the crumbs down with the remains of his drink, Alex rose and fished out his hat from the pile of clothes in the hallway cupboard.

"I'll see you tonight if it's all the same to you."

"Darling, that would be absolutely divine."

GOOD TO HIS word, Alex returned that night and was received with the same warmth as Ida had offered him twenty-four hours earlier. The effusive words didn't quite match how she behaved towards him.

She slumped back on her chaises longue and picked up her pipe, inhaled deeply and then promptly lost herself in an opium haze for two or three hours. The first while, Alex just sat there and enjoyed the tranquility that Ida's intoxication offered, but soon he got bored. The whole point of being with Ida was to share some words and to steal a few moments of joy under the bedclothes.

Thirty minutes into her reverie, Alex grabbed his coat and hit the streets, determined to find a place to eat and to overhear other people's conversations if he wasn't able to engage in talk with his paramour. Perhaps that was the heart of the dilemma—Alex still thought of Ida as a mistress rather than as a girlfriend. Deep down he knew the problem between them couldn't be resolved by changing the name he used to describe her.

Alex wandered the streets for about five minutes before settling on a joint with a line of ten people waiting to get a seat. If nothing else, it showed it was popular—and judging by the decor, the food would be what was selling the restaurant and not its potted plants.

He walked to the front of the line and ignored the scowls from the johns who had been standing for quite some time ahead of him.

"I'm looking for a table."

"Aren't they all, Mac?"

The maître d' was busy scribbling away at his paperwork and failed to look at his customer for their first interaction. Then his eyes moved up Alex's torso until he saw his face.

"Oh, sir, forgive me. I didn't see you standing there."

With a flourish, Benito undid the rope which separated the line from his restaurant interior and Alex stepped through. Although they had never met, the guy recognized Alex on sight. He had purposefully headed toward the outskirts of Little Italy and anyone who valued their business knew who he was—and Anastasia and Louis too.

"I'm afraid there isn't a great selection of tables at present. If you'd been able to book ahead, then we could have been better prepared for you."

"No matter. I am interested in a simple bowl of pasta and then I'll be out of your hair. No need to go to any special effort on my account."

They both knew this was a lie and each man pretended they believed him. When a gang boss enters your establishment, only a fool would treat him like any other customer. So Alex enjoyed a sumptuous three-course meal along with a demi-bottle of red wine. He left a generous tip after Benito waived all charges and went back to the apartment to find Ida was still unconscious.

Alex hovered over her for a minute, trying to decide what he should do. He stared at the burned crumbs around the edge of her pipe and reminded himself of the pleasant hours he had spent lying in a soporific haze with an opium pipe when he was a young man. Those days were long gone and all he saw before him was an addled woman being eaten away from the inside by the opium she smoked. A shell of a person.

He shuddered uncontrollably and turned to leave. That was the moment Ida came to and reached out a hand.

"Get me a drink will you, darling?" she whispered hoarsely and then let her arm flop down again.

He acceded to her request but had no interest in spending much more time with her. Ida was part of his past and he should stop himself from looking back. If he did it too often, then he would turn into a pillar of salt.

21

THE AMERICAN LEGAL system is a wonderful thing and in time-honored tradition, Matt Knowles did exactly what was expected of him—he swung the jury around and Dutch walked free from court. Dewey was none too impressed with the outcome, but he couldn't argue with the decision made by twelve good men and true. Well, eleven and Knowles.

For Dutch, the news was bittersweet—he was pleased to be found not guilty but he wanted revenge on the prosecutor for trying to take him down. Schultz did the only sensible thing that a man in his position could do—he called an extraordinary meeting of the inner circle of the syndicate, with only one item on the agenda.

"Gentlemen, thank you all for coming. I understand this is out of the ordinary, but we live in unusual times."

Charlie offered a benign smile, Meyer stared blankly out of the suite window and the others shuffled papers, inhaled cigarettes, and sipped at their various refreshments. Alex was prepared to listen to the fella, although Albert and Louis seemed disinterested—hard for him to tell for certain.

"Dutch, I am sure I speak for everyone when I say how pleased I am that you have evaded justice and continue to walk free along these hallowed streets in New York. I'd have thought you would want to get back to your business interests rather than sit around and chat with us old men."

This generated a chuckle from the assembled group—all but Dutch, that is.

"Charlie, breathing air as a free man is a wonderful thing, but sometimes that is not enough. Besides, you flatter yourself if you think you are an *alte kaker*. None of you are over the hill—in contrast, you control this city and territories way beyond here too. Don't undersell yourself."

"Dutch, we all know how fortunate we have been in our business enterprises, but unfortunately, I have not been as successful predicting what's in people's minds. Why have you brought us here today?"

"I have a proposal for you all to consider."

Schultz looked around the room in Luciano's hotel suite to gauge the reaction, but these were the hardest men to read in the country. Meyer's bored expression was noticeable, but anyone who knew the man understood he didn't like to let fellas know what he was thinking, so it all could have been a bluff.

"There is a menace in our city and unless we do something, we will be destroyed by it. Maybe not today or tomorrow, but someday and that time is soon."

"It's too late to build an ark and wait for the flood."

Benny's derision oozed out of every syllable, and even Meyer raised an eyebrow before returning to his neutral countenance.

"I don't get why you are all being so flippant. First, they came for Alfonse and we did nothing and they locked him up and threw away the key. Then they put me in their sights and the jury saw fit to dismiss the charges."

Dutch glanced at Alex, but he didn't return the eye contact.

"So the next thing that'll happen is that they come after me again with some more trumped-up accusations or one of you will be taking your turn at the courthouse."

"What are you suggesting, Dutch?"

"We need to kill that cockroach, Thomas Dewey. If we don't slam him under our boots now, that roach'll scurry back again and again until he takes us all down, one after the other."

For the first time since he entered the room, Meyer's expression altered.

"Let me get this straight, you want to hit a special prosecutor because he charged you with tax evasion of which you were wholly guilty?"

"Yes, Meyer."

"And from what I understand, you are only at liberty to come to this meeting due to some help from your friends."

Alex felt Meyer's eyes bear down on him and ignored the implication of the attention he was receiving. Now was not the time to admit in front of witnesses he'd been jury tampering. Not that he had trust issues with any of the fellas in the room—although Louis and Anastasia were on his watch list—but that private matter should remain just that.

"This isn't anything personal—this is business. The longer Dewey sticks around, the more he'll uncover and the harder it will be for us to continue operating as we do. When Prohibition came in, we adapted to take account of the new circumstances. Now Prohibition is ending, we must be prepared to do the same again. Only this time, we need to alter what we do to protect our wealth. I won't remind any of you we are discussing way more than mere chump change."

Charlie's back stiffened and Meyer turned his head and body to face Dutch. Benny continued to slump down in his seat, twiddling a nickel around his fingers. Alex glanced at Albert and Louis and they too had leaned forward now that gelt was being discussed.

"There is nothing wrong in killing a cop if collectively his death is worth millions to us," intoned Dutch.

Albert nodded slowly but Louis tilted his head to one side as Schultz continued. "Why do you think this whack job won't move on to other parts of the country if he doesn't get a big win soon? You know what these federal gumshoes are like."

"The fact he is a cop makes matters difficult but not impossible," Charlie interjected. "But this is not an ordinary policeman on the beat. We can't offer this guy a handful of green and send him on his way. This is a person who has been nominated by Hoover and is a special prosecutor. Correct me if I'm wrong, but nobody has ever put a contract out on a bureau man before. Meyer?"

Lansky shook his head in the negative. "Not to my recollection, Charlie. Besides which, a special prosecutor isn't the same as a district attorney. Those we influence indirectly with our politicians. Dewey is clean. I wouldn't say he's untouchable, but a simple bribe will not work with his sort."

Dutch sighed heavily. "I am not saying we should give him money and tell him to go away. I'm saying we should bury the *goy*—no offense intended."

The Italians in the room were visibly rankled by Schultz's offensive term for non-Jews. Judging by their expressions, Alex couldn't decide if Dutch had got bound up in his own anger and passion or whether he had revealed his genuine distaste for those of other faiths.

Alex broke the tension in the room because everybody's attention had been diverted by Dutch's outburst and he for one needed them to reach a conclusion. He wanted to pop over to Ida on his way home to hand back his key and call it quits with her. He'd finally had enough of that opium head.

"You still haven't explained why Murder Corporation should get a new contract."

"Alex, the situation is very simple. Dewey has attacked me and I demand revenge on him and his family."

Meyer agreed with Alex. "Leave his wife and kids out of this, Dutch. If your complaint is business and nothing personal, then there is no need for citizens to get hurt."

"All right, don't touch the wife and kids, but kill the cop."

"Dutch, I understand you are angry and that is normal," commented Charlie, "but murdering a special prosecutor so soon after he tried to lock you up. Don't you think the cops will come running to your front door before the body is even cold?"

"You seem to believe if we hit Dewey that law enforcement won't take a sharp intake of breath before they do anything like respond. I'm not so sure. If you are right, and hitting a special prosecutor is such a big deal, don't you think they'll hold back from retaliating— they will want to appear all high and mighty."

"And your plan would be to skip town until the heat dies down and leave us to pick up the pieces?" Benny laughed again, even more so when Dutch's expression dramatically shifted to reflect that this was his actual intention.

"After we show what happens to senior cops when they poke their noses in our business, they'll back off. Surely, between us we have enough lawmakers in our pay to see that the squeaky Dewey is sent packing to shove his snout somewhere else, Charlie."

"The politicians who do our bidding are local—Tammany Hall has power, but it's taken a beating since the elections. Besides, with La Guardia as mayor, you know how he will only win more supporters if he uncovers a racket and shuts it down."

Meyer uncrossed his legs and poured himself another glass of water. Tempers were frayed and Alex knew Lansky preferred a calm atmosphere in which to discuss business. The others remained silent to give the financier time to gather his thoughts.

"Dutch, you are right to bring this matter to the syndicate and I commend you for showing this respect. And you are also correct to say that our takings will go up if Dewey leaves us alone or goes away and finds some other itch to scratch."

Dutch smiled, but Meyer raised his palm before adding, "But you are mistaken if you think assassinating the cop will make any difference. These are troubled times for everybody, with La Guardia and Dewey breathing down our necks. You are right to call Dewey a cockroach and like that insect, if you crush one of them then others will appear in their place."

Charlie rose, then paced up and down to stretch his legs.

"Let's put this to a vote. Those in favor of taking out Dewey?"

Dutch's solitary arm rose.

"Those against?"

Every other hand in the room showed opposition to the motion.

"Then we are decided—Dewey lives to fight another day."

As Charlie sat down, Dutch sprang to his feet and stormed out the door. As he turned the handle, they all heard him mutter under his breath, "I'm gonna kill that cockroach."

22

"DID I HEAR him straight?" Charlie looked round the room because he couldn't believe the words he'd just heard.

"Reckon so, and while I don't think now is the right time, Dutch has a point."

All eyes turned to Anastasia, who shrugged at the attention and quizzical expressions on everybody else's faces and took a drag on his cigarette.

"Are you serious?"

"I'm just saying Dewey is bad for business and it is better to rid ourselves of the current problem sooner rather than later. If they send another prosecutor after us, so be it. Meanwhile, it'll take ages for Hoover to appoint a different guy he can trust as much and we should use that time to prepare for the arrival."

Meyer shook his head. "We had a vote and decided. Do we have to rake over the coals again?"

"Who's raking? I am stating that La Guardia might not be so quick to send cops into our neighborhoods if there's a real possibility of a bullet heading in his direction."

"Albert, you started by reminding us you agreed with the decision," hissed Charlie, "So let it go. Now is not the time to attack the police and if Dutch keeps his word, he will take matters into his own hands."

"And that will be bad for business," added Meyer.

"What are we going to do about it?"

Alex's question was well-timed because it was what everyone was asking themselves.

"Shall I run after him and try to change his mind?"

"Thanks for the offer, Louis. Although that hothead might go home now, it doesn't mean he won't hit Dewey tomorrow instead."

"What are you suggesting?

"Nothing at the moment—only that he needs to be stopped."

Charlie sat back in his chair and allowed the others to burst into conversation. Each man had a viewpoint and wanted to express it there and then. Luciano was smart and let them vent until their initial energy had dissipated and a calm descended in the room.

During this time, Alex checked out the decor of Charlie's suite. The penthouse was vast and the boardroom table shone with its recent polishing. Three paintings hung on the walls—all bright colors and country scenes. The furniture comprised leather upholstery and Alex imagined the bedroom contained a four-poster bed.

He was brought back to reality by Charlie's voice. His friend had brought matters to order otherwise they'd have spent the rest of the day jawing and achieving nothing.

"Sounds to me we agree that we should not allow Dutch to take out the prosecutor."

Nods all round, although Albert's head appeared the most reluctant.

"What do you propose we do about it, Charlie?"

"Albert, that is for us to discuss and then decide."

"Then let's give him a well-deserved break. Send him to Florida for a vacation. The weather might not be great, but he could spend some time in the casinos, meet some new girls—he'll be away from all this *tsoris* and we deal with Dewey in a more mature way."

"Meyer, a few weeks out of the city will do Dutch some good—but will it be enough to stop him?"

"What do you mean, Alex?"

"Assuming we can get Dutch to agree to pack up and leave Manhattan for a month, do you really think that would prevent him getting Abe Landau or Bernard Rosenkrantz to do his dirty work? They are fiercely loyal as his lieutenants should be."

"You saying we should force them on vacation too?"

"Meyer, that isn't realistic. We can't send the top tier of Dutch's crew away. How would his business survive?"

"So what are you suggesting, Alex?"

"Albert, I'm not sure—I am concerned that Meyer's suggestion won't work, but I don't have a solution to our problem."

"Meanwhile, he could march over to Dewey's office to put a bullet through his brains."

Albert uttered their biggest fear. If Dutch carried through with his threat—and everyone expected he would, sooner or later—then the heat that would rain down on them would be intense. Alex gathered his thoughts and followed the logic of Albert's statement.

"So we need to prevent Dutch from taking action—in the short term at the very least—and a vacation is not the answer."

"Do you think he's on his way over to Dewey as we sit here and yak?"

"Benny, if he is then we have no way to stop him at all—and this talk will cost us dear. If not then we must do something, if only we could agree what that was."

Charlie was right. Better they spend time and reach a sensible conclusion than behave like hotheads with itchy trigger fingers.

"Should we take him and offer him a forced vacation—as a guest of one of us out of town?"

"You mean kidnap him, Meyer?"

"Yes, Albert, if you must put it that way."

"Kidnapping will not work. At some point, we'll have to release him and then he will hit Dewey, anyway. I should know—I've worked with him longer than any of you."

Louis was right. Dutch would never let this go—it would chew up his insides until he burst.

"What's left?"

Louis looked straight into Charlie's eyes.

"There is only one option—Dutch must die."

◆ ◆ ◆

FOR THE FIRST time that anyone could remember, somebody suggested killing one of their own. That the words fell out of Louis' lips made the moment even more poignant. He and Dutch had grown up together, played together, robbed together, strong-armed and assaulted together until they became bosses and members of the syndicate.

"Is there any need for bloodshed?"

"Meyer, your desire to solve all problems through discussion and contemplation is admirable, but sometimes a drop or two of blood has to flow."

Louis went silent, staring into his lap, adjusting himself to the possibility that Dutch Schultz would be killed by a man in the room. Alex tried to think if there was any other way out of this mess.

"It's us or him," noted Benny with no trace of emotion in his voice. He swallowed, and Alex wondered whether Siegel was hoping to have the honor of killing the fella. Him rather than me, determined Alex at the prospect of gunning down a commissioner in the syndicate. Albert sighed, sipped at his drink, and leaned back in his chair, mimicking Charlie.

"What other choice do we have? I think Dewey should be offed, only not now. We cannot be seen to allow fellas to fly around and do whatever they want. We have organizations to run and can't afford to have guys doing whatever they feel like. Even though the man has a point, he is going about this the wrong way and we need to stop him—and fast."

Louis continued to stare at his knees, refusing to acknowledge the discussion taking place around him. Meyer scratched his head, hoping an alternative might spring to mind. "I'd still like us to consider holding him against his will until he sees reason."

Benny laughed. "And how many years do you think it'll take before we can set him free? Get real. Dutch isn't a fella to change his opinion when he has fixed on an idea. Right, Louis?"

Louis looked up and nodded.

"His head is never for turning. Once he's decided, that's it until the day he dies."

"An unfortunate choice of words. Are you telling us we must kill him?"

Louis stared into Albert's eyes until he looked no more. He knew the answer and despite Meyer's hopes for a peaceful settlement, there was no way out that any of them could see.

"Any other proposals on the table?" Charlie asked, more as a formality than in the belief that anybody would step forward with a better suggestion. "Then let's put it to a vote, unless anyone wants to say anything first?"

Silence.

"Those in favor of clipping Dutch Schultz?"

Every hand rose—even Louis' because it was the right thing to do.

Charlie nodded without verbalizing what they had witnessed. "Let's break for a bite to eat. We all could do with getting out of the place and settling our stomachs."

THEY WALKED DOWN to the restaurant and into a private dining room. Albert, Louis, and Alex were only too aware they had a new contract and someone would have to follow through with it. Alex just hoped it wasn't going to be him.

A steak and fries later and he hadn't changed his mind. Charlie ensured the conversation didn't linger on Schultz all the time, but he was never far from any of their thoughts. Benny seized the opportunity to be the center of attention and cracked a series of funny gags, which made everyone laugh.

"We normally leave you guys to manage your own business but this isn't a usual hit. Which Murder Corporation executive will do the deed?"

The three men glanced at each other—no one wanted to volunteer.

"You two have known him far longer than me…"

"Does that mean it should be you as you have a weaker connection with him, Alex?"

"Albert, I did a favor for Schultz recently, so let's not play that game."

Anastasia shrugged and chewed on his chicken. Louis stuffed himself with his pastrami sandwich and refused to be so rude as to talk with his mouth full. Benny chuckled, shook his head, and enjoyed the scene. Everyone understood he'd happily whack the fella if anybody bothered to ask him, but this discussion wasn't so much about getting the job done as seeing who would be prepared to clip the guy. Finally Albert broke the silence. "It should be Louis. They go back and we can trust he'll do it decently—with respect."

"Only if I have Alex as a witness. I don't want any bums telling me I didn't follow through on my word."

Before Alex had a chance to complain, the matter was settled.

23

LOUIS AND ALEX told their respective lieutenants they wanted to know when anybody spotted Schultz and the next day Massimo reported he'd been seen in Newark, so the two headed off through the tunnel and hoped they'd figure out a plan before they met up with him.

Once in New Jersey, they switched cars so no one would look twice at their local plates—not that a New York vehicle was such a rare sight in the neighboring state. Caution was the word and using the same getaway car all the way into the city would have been a monumental mistake.

They drove round town randomly switching from street to street in case they bumped into Schultz, but after fifteen minutes they stopped and Alex hopped out to place a call.

"Massimo, any more news about our target?"

"Nothing certain, but his favorite Chinese restaurant can't be far from you. I don't know if you've noticed the time but I reckon you'll find Dutch at the Palace Chop House."

"You got an address for me? Newark is not my town."

"It's on East Park Street. Be careful because the joint is popular and there could be several citizens in there."

"Thanks for the warning."

Back in the limousine, Louis knew the place and, with a squeal, he lurched the vehicle toward Schultz's demise.

"WHAT'S YOUR PLAN?"

Louis parked the car around the corner from the restaurant and Alex relaxed into his seat, while Louis gripped the steering wheel like it was about to fly out of the window. Alex needed the guy to be much calmer before the hit could begin.

"My mind's blank, Alex. I can't imagine a single thing to do to murder my friend."

"You could burst through the entrance and blast your way to his table?"

"And shoot Dutch in the face while he's eating? What kind of person do you think I am?"

"You're a fella with a hit to carry out. It is not about how you feel that matters, but what you have been contracted to do."

"Easy for you to say."

"I've killed my fair share of friends, Louis—you have no idea."

They were both quiet for a spell as Louis remained locked to the wheel and Alex's mind flitted briefly to Sammy, the guy who'd introduced him to Waxey Gordon.

A truck backfired in the distance and Alex bounced back into the present day. He turned to check out Louis and saw the fella frozen to the spot—unmoved from the minute he pulled the car over and parked. Alex sighed because he experienced a sinking feeling in his stomach as he realized what would happen.

"Are you able to go through with this?"

"Maybe… I don't know. Honestly, I'm not sure I can do it."

"What are you saying?"

Louis exhaled and swallowed before responding.

"Will you carry out the job for me?"

Alex had figured this moment would come and deep within he didn't want to admit to himself that he had known from before they left Midtown.

"I guess I must."

Louis nodded, still unable to look Alex square in the face.

"Then I shall."

As soon as Louis heard Alex's agreement, he released his grip on the steering wheel and the tension seemed to ebb from his shoulders. They remained in the car for five minutes until Alex decided he'd had enough and resolved to walk around the block.

ALEX KEPT HIS hands in his pants pockets and his head down as he wandered the Newark streets. He couldn't stay in the same cage with Louis for another moment. After a few minutes air, he didn't so much have a plan as he'd cleared his mind enough to know that the best way was to try for a rear entrance and play it by ear from that point on. The only thing he was certain of—Louis would not be joining him and he hoped the guy could function as a getaway driver otherwise he was a total waste of space.

When Alex arrived back by the car, he looked round to get his bearings, nodded at Louis who was enjoying a cigarette, and vanished into the evening as he took a long arc before arriving at the rear of the Palace Chop House. There were two large dumpsters six feet away from a rear glass door. As he approached, Alex saw there were also boxes next to the wall between the nearest dumpster and the doorway. In the dim light, he thought he made out some movement by the entrance, but couldn't see well enough to know exactly what was going on inside.

ALEX SIDLED FORWARD until his back slammed against the brickwork with the door to his left. He pulled out his pistol but kept it by his side. There was no point having a gun fight if all he had seen was a citizen heading for the john. He waited thirty seconds, ears pricked keenly, hoping to make out what was happening indoors. There were two muffled voices inches away from him, but he couldn't make out a single thing they said to each other.

A big exhalation and Alex edged closer to the handle and reached out just as the door swung open and a man in a tall white cylindrical hat walked out and strode six paces forward. The door remained still for a moment, shutting slowly to reveal Alex, but the cook hadn't seen him because the guy hadn't looked around. He stood, legs apart, inhaling his cigarette without a care in the world.

With his pistol returned to his jacket pocket, Alex strode four giant steps and put one palm over the guy's mouth, dragging him back toward the wall. A punch to the kidneys with his free hand and the cook scrunched into a little ball. A kick in the head as he lay on the ground and the man stopped moving. Alex checked his pulse—still alive—and opened the nearest dumpster and tipped the slumped body out of the way. He'd be fine when he eventually came to, although the stench of his surroundings would not be to his pleasing.

Back to the entrance and Alex could tell there was nobody on the other side, so he twisted the handle and pulled the door ajar. There were still no sounds nearby, so he opened the door fully and whipped inside.

He was in a corridor. At the far end was the main restaurant—he made out some white tablecloths with diners seated around them. Between him and the customers were two doors either side by the exit, clearly labeled as the washrooms for men and women. Five feet further up were another pair of doors. One was only an archway which led into the kitchen and the other was closed and marked as private for office staff only.

Alex considered checking it out, but Dutch was most unlikely to be there—and that was who he was after. So he darted past the kitchen, hustled to the end of the corridor, and peered around the joint. A moment's glance told him that Schultz was not in view, but the space was L-shaped which meant the fella was round the other leg, near the front entrance, out of sight for now.

Another check across the room and still there was nobody Alex recognized. As Schultz would not be dining alone, there must be a welcoming party round the corner and Alex wondered whether he should get Louis to double up the firepower.

He noticed a john stare at him and beckon him over. Alex grabbed a white napkin and draped it over his lower arm. Then he stepped forward.

"Another bottle of wine, waiter."

"Same as before, sir?"

"Yeah, the house red."

"Straight away, sir."

Now he was squarely in the room, Alex made his way forward ostensibly on the hunt for some vino. He reached the corner and returned his pistol to his palm. Deep breath and walk… into nothing. There were six tables in front of him, but Schultz sat at none of them.

Luckily, Alex spotted three faces he'd seen before so he went straight up to Abe Landau, Bernard Rosenkrantz and Otto Berman. The first two fellas would pack heat and the third one was a pencil pusher and was harmless. Bernard looked up at Alex and his jaw dropped open.

"Any of you birds seen Dutch around?"

"What the…?"

Otto responded but noticed the other two were stony silent, so he halted in mid-sentence. His eyes glanced back in the direction Alex had just come, while the others said nothing and very visibly kept their hands on the table, silverware down, palms facing the tablecloth. As passive and as calming as they could be.

Abe was the first to make a move and tried to stand up and pull a gun from out of his jacket. More fool him, because Alex squeezed a bullet into his right lung before both legs were straight. Bernard lurched sideways and tried to roll onto the floor, but Alex was too quick for him and pulled the trigger a second time, grazing Bernard's leg with the slug.

Like everybody else in the restaurant, Otto let out a scream but was the only person in the joint to stay perfectly still. Despite being an accountant, his desperate desire to live forced him to do the only sensible thing—remain motionless so he couldn't be hit by any stray bullet.

Alex pulled their table out of his way, causing chow mein to fly in all directions. This gave him the opportunity to fire a second shot into Abe at even closer range—this time in the head. Bernard tried to squirm around, but Alex fired at his kneecap.

With the room in uproar, Alex stood up straight and ensured every civilian got a good look at his piece—nobody would make the mistake of trying to be a hero.

"Everybody onto the ground."

This simple instruction was followed by half the johns and the rest sat and stared, not sure what to do, unable to believe they were sitting amid a gun battle when all they had been expecting was crispy fried duck.

Alex worked his way back toward the rear of the joint until he reached the corridor. Still no sign of Schultz. A quick check in the kitchen revealed nothing but scared chefs and waiters. He used the barrel of his gun to show that everyone needed to stay where they were—and no one looked like they had any other plans.

Then it struck him—there were two places Alex hadn't tried. He stormed down the corridor and into the men's washroom. Nothing. He kicked open the two cubicles, but there was nobody to be found.

Back to the office and inside was a solitary man, cowering behind his desk. The manager had stayed put—Alex couldn't tell if it was out of fear or good sense. Alex placed a finger in front of his lips to insist on silence and ripped the phone cord out of its socket and left.

Perhaps Schultz had somehow doubled back on him and escaped out the rear while Alex searched in the front. If so, he was wasting his time creating all this mayhem and needed to get out before the cops came flying in. Good job Alex had the presence of mind to put a kerchief over his face before firing the first shot.

Alex was about to leave when he discerned a noise from the women's washroom. He smiled because he knew what he would find even before he'd opened the door. But when he did, there was nobody there and just a bar of soap languishing on the otherwise clean floor. An empty room with two washbasins and three cubicles with all the partition doors closed.

He padded in and bent down to peek below the bottom of each of the cubicle doors. There was nothing but a toilet base to be seen in two of them, but the middle booth contained a pair of shoes. Men's shoes. Alex grinned, quietly entered one of the other cubicles and stepped up onto the toilet. There was Schultz, sat down, ear craning forward, trying to hear whatever was going on outside that cubicle space.

Alex let out a sigh which made Schultz turn round, but he failed to glance up. Alex fired twice at the fella until he fell off his perch and smashed onto the floor—his body wedged between the door and the toilet base. Alex dropped a third shot into Schultz's torso just to be certain he wouldn't survive. Then he exited the building and ran a block south before circling back to reach Louis' car.

"Get out of here."

"Thanks, Alex."

"Just drive, will you?"

24

THAT WEEKEND, ALEX made sure to spend some time with his boys. He felt as though he hadn't seen them for months, which was probably true. Funny thing was that he genuinely wanted to be there for them, although he found it hard to keep his word.

He called them boys because that was the age they were fixed in his head—and this reflected how little he actually saw of them. But the eldest were in their teens and beginning to get pimply. Moishe had grown himself a squarish man-jaw and David's limbs were barely under his control right now.

Asher, Elijah, and Arik were still prepared to play childish games with him, but Alex knew that within the next year or two, they would tire of this also and morph into young men. He had bought an apartment near to where they lived so they would have somewhere solid to come to when they were visiting him.

This was his New Jersey crash pad, but he tried to maintain it solely for the family. When he was entertaining out of town, he'd stay in a hotel rather than use this place for female company. It was almost as though he sensed the spirit of Sarah inside these walls, channeled by his four sons.

The irony was not lost on Alex that despite this, Sarah never came up into the apartment itself—the concierge would always call up for her and Ezra or Massimo would walk them out to the elevator and take them safely to the lobby.

This Sunday it was getting late—heading toward five in the evening, and Alex was wondering when he could head return to the city. The two eldest were becoming tetchy because the other three were proving insufferable—he should have listened to himself an hour ago and taken them out to the park to run them ragged. Instead they needed feeding–Alex knew there was not nearly enough food in the icebox to satisfy all these hungry mouths.

He was about to ask if they'd like to go for a Chinese when the buzzer rang. Alex let Ezra check who it was and, to his surprise, in walked Sarah. She smiled and headed toward him, landing a peck on the cheek.

"Good to see you, Sarah."

"Likewise, Alex. How have the boys been?"

"A bundle of fun—but I don't have to tell you that."

"Well they can be a riot, but I'm the one who has to set the rules and make them follow them."

"You do a fabulous job with the kids. They need to have a strong guiding hand so they grow up with a solid moral compass."

"Given who their parents are, I can't see that happening."

They chuckled because a nafka and a gangster were not everybody's idea of role models.

"We haven't done so bad by them, all things considered."

"Maybe not, Alex. Even so…"

Alex couldn't face a conversation which would take them on a journey through their failings as parents. He'd experienced this dialog before and he always finished up on the receiving end of Sarah's rebuking tongue—he didn't want that to be how his day with the boys finished. Besides, how often had Sarah been to the apartment?

"Would you like to be taken on the grand tour—I don't think you've seen this place before, have you?"

"That'd be nice. And yes, this is my first time here."

"Well, the children have always been able to pop down when you rang, haven't they?"

Sarah nodded, although they both understood she could have done the same thing this evening, only there must be a reason for her change in behavior.

Alex took her from one room to the next—the five bedrooms, spacious living area, kitchen and three bathrooms. Few men could afford a place as big as this, she thought.

Sarah had never judged Alex poorly for the manner in which he earned his money but resented his dishonesty over Ida and the way his business had put her and, more importantly, the children in danger. There was no excuse for either of those things.

They returned to the living room to find the younger boys in tears and the two oldest sat on the couch in abject silence.

"I'd better get these fellas fed."

"We could all go to a restaurant, if you fancied?"

"That's kind, Alex, but I'll say no thank you."

He must have showed how his hopes had been let down because Sarah added an unusual question.

"I don't suppose you might be free one evening this week? I'd like to talk to you about something and not have the children running around."

"Sure, pick a day. Any is good for me."

Alex wondered what was so important that she was prepared to meet up with him without the excuse of the boys, but deep down he knew the reason.

"I WANT A divorce, Alex."

He sat opposite her for their second meal together since she'd walked out on him all those years ago. It was like it had been yesterday, or rather that's how it seemed to him. Sarah clearly had a different experience of the intervening time.

Alex pretended not to have heard her, but they both knew this was not the case. He continued to chew his salmon, although Sarah had put her silverware down.

"This is good, don't you think?"

"Please don't change the subject on me, Alex. If what we had together meant anything to you, I deserve better than to be ignored."

She was right and he swallowed and stopped pretending to focus on his plate.

"What do you expect me to say?"

"Yes, of course. We have been apart for quite a while now."

Five and a half years, he thought, without needing to count.

"And I hate to break it to you, but there are no signs we are getting back together soon."

Alex clenched his molars because that was probably the only sentence in the world he didn't want to hear. Despite all he had done —and not done—he'd harbored the belief that one day, somehow, he and Sarah would live together again. That her departure was a blip and that he would someday sleep under the same roof as his boys. Now Sarah had uttered those words, the chances of his fervent wish coming true seemed as distant as the moon.

"I thought one day…"

"Really, Alex? Would you say anything has changed between us since I left?"

"I don't lie to you anymore. I have only spoken the truth. That much I owed you and you made it clear to me that was the reason you had to leave."

"Alex, babe. Yes, you have kept your word to me—about who you spend your time with. And I appreciate it—I do, but…"

She looked into his doleful eyes and realized how much she was hurting him, so she paused. Alex grabbed his water glass and took a few sips to quench his parched lips. Then he swiped his right eye with the back of his palm.

"…but we need to move on. You will always be the boys' father— and you are a wonderful provider even though they don't spend time with you as regularly as they would like."

"Or as often as I'd want too," Alex interjected.

"As adults we have drifted apart and that is only natural under the circumstances."

"I still feel close to you, Sarah."

"Huh? We've spoken only a handful of times and almost every time it has been about a kid."

"Maybe, I figured…"

"You figured wrong, Alex. We have both moved on and I'd like to make it official."

The word stuck in his craw. Raised a flag in his mind, although he was fighting back emotions he had stifled for so long now. He thought for a minute and understood the entire picture. What a fool he had been.

"Do you want to marry someone else?"

"Don't you want to settle down with somebody and not spend all your effort on those *shayner maidel* half your age I read about in the papers?"

"They've meant nothing to me. I was waiting for you to come back to me and just wanted some warmth in my bed."

"And I don't suppose Ida is still on the scene, is she?"

"Yes and no. I hardly see her and every time I do, I ask myself why I bother. It's laziness on my part—and punishment in equal measure."

"I'm not coming back to you, Alex. Divorce me and set me free, please."

Suddenly there was an edge to Sarah's voice—like she had tried to play nicely and now she just wanted to get the job done. It was the tone he imagined she would use on the children. Commanding. Assertive.

Precisely the approach which made him react with disgust that she should try that on him. He might have skulked about behind her back with that actress, but he had always treated Sarah with respect. He'd gone from tipping her ten bucks for a night under the covers to giving her five strapping sons. And this was how she would treat him.

"No divorce, Sarah. And no further discussion on the matter. We either finish our meal or you can walk away now. The choice is yours, but we will remain married. Do you hear?"

25

ALEX WAS STILL recoiling from the previous night's dinner conversation the following morning when Albert asked him to handle a job in Bed-Stuy, which was much closer to his beloved Midtown than Alex might have expected.

"The location might be local but the target is not—he's over from Philadelphia, hiding from a bunch of problems he hopes will go away by the time he returns…"

"…but, Albert, when he arrives home he'll be in a wooden box."

"Nicely put, Alex."

"You're welcome. Tell me more about the contract as I don't remember us discussing this one at our last meeting."

"The situation was urgent so Charlie, Louis, Meyer and Benny voted it through over the weekend. You were out of town, as I understand."

Alex nodded, concerned about what else had happened in his absence that he had no idea about. Was Albert scheming behind his back? That thought had no time to roost while Anastasia explained the situation.

"Huxley Cole left his hometown on Friday evening after a disagreement with a lieutenant."

"What was the nature of their discussion?"

"Luca Marchesi had a difference of opinion with Huxley over how he treated the girls he dated."

"I didn't think lieutenants bothered themselves over such matters."

"I never did, but we might change our minds if we'd found out that the boy Cole was messing around with was our daughter."

"How old?"

"Eighteen, but still…"

"So Luca wanted Huxley to leave the apple of his eye alone."

"And then some. If they'd been on a date or two behind her father's back then that would have been the end of it. The trouble was that they had got intimate and our boy Cole had yet to discover how to be gentle and caring with the women he slept with."

"You mean he got rough?"

"And some, from what we understand. The girl's a mess and Luca wants blood."

"The fact he is holed up in Brooklyn shows he knows how much trouble he's put himself in."

"My sources tell me he is staying with friends. Two troublemakers who've been a thorn in my side in their time."

"So why don't you deal with this situation, instead of dragging me into it?"

"Simple, really, Alex. If either of the other pair are caught in the crossfire, I can't be seen to have pulled the trigger. Don't get me wrong, I'll sleep easy tonight if both of the other guys get theirs."

Then Albert shrugged, not needing to explain to Alex how he wanted the other two hit as a favor as well as Huxley Cole, which was business.

A QUICK DRIVE around the neighborhood and Alex found the right apartment—Albert had supplied him with the address. There were at least three guys inside he could be sure of, maybe more—along with Huxley was Piero Buffone and Samuele Gallo.

Alex parked his stolen car around the corner and checked the number at the entrance before he walked in and went up the two flights to reach apartment D, Gallo's joint. He knocked on the door and readied himself for anything that might happen. As always in these situations, a lifetime later a guy in a bathrobe appeared at the threshold, stood with his hand on the handle. Alex eyed him up and down, trying to judge the measure of him and attempting to figure out why he answered the door at all.

"The landlord sent me. I need to check the windows."

"We're kinda busy, pop. Can't you come back later?"

"Nah, I have to get this done today. Landlord said so."

"If you have to then make yourself at home."

The boy sniggered slightly as he spoke and Alex wondered what was so funny. He followed the guy into the living room and got the joke. There were two other men and three women in various states of undress lying on top of or squatting near each other. It might have only been the middle of the afternoon, but the partying had definitely started before lunch.

Alex tipped his hat—he couldn't think of anything else to do—and zigzagged around the limbs and torsos until he got to the window and pushed and pulled at the sash, pretending to know something about fenestration. Even the guy with the robe had stopped watching him and had returned to more fleshy pursuits.

Still with his back to the group, Alex looked out on the street and noticed a pretzel and hotdog booth but not much else of interest down below. The fire escape came into focus as his near vision kicked in and he thought about how he would get the job done. He shut his eyes for a second and wished there were fewer people in the apartment.

When he opened them two seconds later, the same number of bodies lay in the living room, but at least Alex knew what he would do. He swiveled round and used the time to whip out his gun. He raised his arm and wielded the piece at Huxley. Just as he squeezed the trigger, a breast appeared in the periphery of his vision and he lost concentration. The bullet whizzed past Huxley's ear and lodged in the wall behind him.

The boy ducked down, pushing the woman kneeling in between his legs onto her back on the ground. She hit her head on a nearby table and called out in pain. Gallo and Buffone looked up at the commotion and only saw the girl lying on the floor.

Alex swallowed and stared straight at Huxley and fired three bullets into his torso, causing his body to flail against the wall and then slump back onto the armchair he had originally been sitting on. The two remaining living men stood up and searched around to find their pieces, but wherever they were, both guys realized their clothes were all jumbled up in their girls' underwear with their guns buried somewhere in that mess.

As Alex had moved into the center of the room to guarantee he hit Huxley, Gallo bolted for the window and Buffone headed for the exit. Watching their men fly in different directions, the girls remained on the floor for a moment before experiencing that deep pit of dread and fear that launched them upwards, screaming. Both women fled for the door knowing they needed to create as much distance as possible between themselves and the stranger with the gun.

They reached the entrance at exactly the same time as Buffone. He yanked one head out of the way and pushed the other girl onto the floor. The gentleman then ran the three paces across the hallway, almost ripped the front door off its hinges and hustled down the stairs. Once they got to their feet, the girls followed him out.

Meantime, Gallo had flung open the sash window and was out on the fire escape. Luckily for him, New York was experiencing a warm fall because Alex watched him fly downwards, as naked as the day he was born. Alex swore under his breath because he knew he couldn't walk away from the nude mayhem he had sent out onto the streets of Brooklyn.

He popped his head out of the window to see that Gallo was still on the fire escape, slowed down by the rough surface of the metal steps on the soles of his bare feet. Alex sighed and followed the boy onto the ladder and down.

GALLO REACHED THE second floor by the time Alex was out on the fire ladder. The boy heard Alex's arrival on the metal steps—looked up, stared down—and leaped to the sidewalk rather than take the slower route of descending the steps farther. Despite his best intentions, Gallo landed badly and gripped his ankle, giving Alex the chance to catch up.

Before the boy could rise to his feet, Alex hurried down the ladder and dropped onto the sidewalk next to the guy. Revolver out, Alex put one slug in his chest and another between the eyes, then he reloaded from a bunch of loose slugs in his jacket pocket.

A noise made him swivel round. The apartment block entrance burst open and Buffone appeared, took a look at Alex, and hightailed it in the opposite direction. Four seconds later and the two girls emerged, whimpering and yelping, onto the street.

Alex thought about dropping them there and then, but they hugged each other, halted by the entranceway. Instead, Buffone needed to be stopped. Setting off at a trot, Alex followed the naked guy round the corner and reckoned he spotted a bare heel vanish into an alleyway.

Cornered, his quarry attempted to scramble up a fence at the far end of the alley. Finding a firm foothold was tricky as Buffone took four attempts to launch himself to a point where one hand got purchase on the top of the railing. Alex held his gun in both hands and aimed squarely in the middle of the back. Three shots and Buffone fell onto the dirt.

Alex checked his pistol and put a palm up to his mouth. Then he slapped his cheek—the kerchief he usually used to hide his face was still in his pants. He needed to find the two girls before they escaped.

He sprinted back to the apartment block and was lucky—the women hadn't had time to get to their senses and run off. Alex was only fifteen feet away when he shot both of them, one slug each. After they dropped to the ground, he continued to walk toward them and when he was stood right by them, he put two more bullets in both their bodies.

A quick check in both directions and Alex ensured there were no witnesses on the street—except for the pretzel and hotdog concession. He couldn't make out anyone there at first, but as he stared a little more and walked in its direction, Alex reckoned he spotted someone cowering behind the wooden structure.

"Give me a pretzel, will you?"

"Wh… what?"

"You heard me. Can I buy one?"

"Sure thing, mister."

The vendor scooped up a breaded ring and handed it over to Alex, who thanked him and offered a dollar bill as payment. The guy lowered his head to find the correct change and that was the moment Alex planted a bullet in the only witness to his slaughter. He chewed on his snack, headed over to his car and left Bed-Stuy, always traveling below the speed limit. Today was not the day to be stopped by some dumb traffic cop. Despite the vows he'd made to himself, Alex decided the best place for him to be right now was in Ida's suite —a hideout with room service and a warm body in the bed.

26

FOUR DAYS LATER, Alex left the confines of Ida's apartment and spent another week in Hoboken to be near his boys—and to be out of the state should any flatfeet come calling. The furore over the bloodshed had died down in the press—there are only so many times you can put tasteful pictures of naked corpses on your front page. Besides, the syndicate applied pressure on the newspaper owners to give it a rest. There were more important matters for Joe Citizen to worry about than the slaying of a rapist caught in the middle of an orgy, surely?

Alex returned to the city and hunkered down, keeping out of the public eye. He resented the attention the hit received and couldn't decide who he blamed more: Anastasia for putting him onto the gig in the first place or Sarah's request for a divorce that meant his head wasn't in the game when it should have been.

New York moved toward Thanksgiving and the world forgot all about Huxley Cole. Not Alex, but everyone else.

"Charlie, what you think about Albert?"

They had just sat down in the back row of the 44th Street Picture Palace watching a Western because Charlie wanted to see the latest *Hopalong* movie. The film had yet to start and they'd begun munching through their popcorn.

"Can't we simply enjoy the show?"

"Seriously, Charlie. I know he's got Sicilian protection, but don't you think he…?"

"Leave it be, Alex. He is who he is and nothing will change that. The man has a certain way about him—when he gets an idea in his skull, he is like a bull."

"Do you trust him?"

Charlie turned to look at Alex in the flickering light offered by the film projector.

"You kidding me? I count my fingers every time we shake hands."

Alex nodded and settled into his seat as the opening credits burst onto the screen and William Boyd appeared in glorious black and white.

LATER THEY WENT round the corner to a local diner to get a bite to eat. How were they able to walk so freely and safely around Midtown? Bodyguards flanked them the entire evening. A burger and fries each, and the two men sipped at their coffees.

"Alex, I've got a proposition for you."

"What gives?"

"I'd like to make you a fifty-fifty partner in some of my heroin interests in Brooklyn."

"Thank you, but why bestow this honor on me when you don't appear to need any help working this business. Besides, I thought we were focused on East Harlem and Midtown?"

"We are right now, but you always gotta look ahead. You should play checkers—it helps you think about your move after next. If I was smart enough, I'd learn chess."

"We're going to sell to our own in Brownsville?"

"That's not what I said. I'm offering you a half stake in the territory."

"It's filled with hard-working Jews. They don't have time to visit a crummy street corner and buy a packet of dope."

"No, but as they get richer, they'll move away from those street corners and another group of immigrants will arrive instead. Recall what's happened to the Bowery in our lifetimes. Before we arrived, there were the Germans and the Irish. Now the Jews and Italians and who knows who'll turn up next. My point is that we need to be ready when they do."

"And why now?"

"Well, to be honest I must liquidate some assets."

"Huh?"

"Meyer thinks it best for me to have some spending money available at short notice. So I'm asking for you to pay for your stake upfront."

"You want me to give you gelt to sell heroin to people who haven't even moved into the neighborhood yet?"

"That's the short of it, Alex."

"You're *meshugge*."

"I'm not crazy. This is a brilliant opportunity to invest a million dollars into the future."

"How much?" Alex's speedy retort reflected his surprise at the size of the number.

"A million."

"That's a lot of tomorrows you need me to buy today."

"It's an investment—like on Wall Street, only with those shysters the chances are you won't get your money back, let alone receive any return."

"And I suppose they will always want heroin in Bed-Stuy?"

"There's been a steady set of customers ever since I brought the powder into the country a decade ago."

Alex hadn't considered that point before—Charlie had seen the opportunity in heroin before anybody else. It had only just been criminalized when he first talked to Alex about it. The fella sure was good at seeing the move after next.

"We live together, we work together. Right?"

"I'm no Albert Anastasia. When have I ever offered you a bum steer?"

"You've always been true, Charlie. Where did the number of a million spring from?"

"That's all Meyer's doing. I will need to take care of some other affairs of mine and he estimates that'll cost me a seven-digit sum."

"If you don't mind me asking, who's the beef with that you won't use Murder Corporation to sort out?"

"Dewey."

Alex's blood ran cold at the sound of that name.

"We've only heard bupkis from him since the Schultz business."

"That doesn't mean he's put his feet up and stayed at home, Alex. He and his squad have been working through paperwork—Dutch's tax was only the first on their list. My informants tell me that Dewey has his eye on me next."

"And who else?"

"All of us, ultimately. Nobody will escape his attention, Alex."

"Are you paying somebody from out of town to hit him for a million bucks? I'll do it for half that."

Charlie laughed and allowed the mirth to ebb from his body over the course of thirty seconds.

"I'm not going to take Dewey down, but I will pay someone to make the problem go away—I am buying me a top-notch lawyer."

Alex whistled because that was a colossal amount of money for a fella in a suit to earn just by talking.

"And they call *us* robbers, Charlie."

"Yeah, but this guy, Mendy Greenberg reckons he can get me off with no jail time, no matter what I have done."

"That is worth a million of anybody's gelt—and it looks like it will be mine."

"Thank you, Alex. I won't forget this."

THEY LEFT THE diner and headed to Charlie's place for a nightcap. Their entourage stood waiting by the curb before either man stepped onto the sidewalk and into the building.

At the back of the first floor Waldorf Astoria bar, they sat at Charlie's table nursing a Scotch on the rocks each. Massimo, Ezra, and Charlie's people surrounded them, but only drank coffee—they were on duty and had to keep their wits about them. Besides, drinking heavily was for saps—they all knew that.

"So what's the catch, Charlie? Apart from handing over a vast amount of money."

"Nothing, Alex. Why do you insult me by acting as though I am out to get you in some manner?"

"No disrespect intended, Charlie. I've received many gifts from you over the years and you have only ever treated me swell, but other fellas I have worked with in the syndicate have made me cautious, perhaps unnecessarily so."

"Not everybody is like Albert. He's one of a kind. No, the only thing I want you to do is to carry on working with the fella."

"Keep with Murder Corporation, you mean?"

"Yes, right now I need everything to be as calm as possible. If I am correct and Dewey guns for us, then we must all be focused on that threat and not spend any energy having to watch our backs. This is a time for unity."

"You trust him enough for me to believe he won't wake up one morning and cut my throat?"

"There are no certainties in this world, Alex. All we know is that we live together, we work together…"

"…and we die alone."

April 1936

27

THE SAME REAR table in the same bar in the same hotel, but when Alex and Charlie met six months later, the atmosphere had changed —not with Alex, but Charlie's demeanor had altered. The fella was downcast, shoulders sagged and eyes looked like needle points.

"How are you holding up, Charlie?"

"Soon I'll have my day in court."

"You expected Dewey to hit you for tax fraud, not this."

"Yeah, pandering. What the hell is that supposed to be?"

Dewey hadn't bothered going after Charlie over misgotten gelt because there was an easier way to put him behind bars. Like so many other members of the syndicate, Charlie owned a string of cathouses across several boroughs.

Each of them generated income and operated within a strict hierarchy—from nafka to timekeeper, from the brothel owner up through the ranks to Charlie. He might have tried to create a shield between himself and the rest of the operation, but it didn't take Dewey very long to follow the trail and build a case against him.

"They let you out on bail?"

"Mendy worked his magic in front of the judge so I wouldn't have to spend time in Rikers."

"And you think he'll be able to get you off?"

"He's good, but I don't know if he's that good. I can be sure I'm paying him enough to guarantee the guy is focused on my trial and no one else's."

Alex shot a glance directly at Charlie, because they both knew where the funding for the legal eagle had come from.

"How long have you got before the case begins?"

"Two weeks. It's ridiculous. I have all these business matters to attend to but every time I walk out of a joint, there's another gumshoe putting out his cigarette and following me down the road."

"Surely your guys can convince the cops to beat it."

"These are special operations cops—hired by Dewey personally— they are beyond reproach. I haven't been able to bribe one of them since the start of this whole caper. Not one."

"If a detective died in mysterious, violent and public circumstances, that'd send a message."

"Alex, do not even think about joking over such a thing. You don't get it. I am under constant surveillance—as is everyone I come into contact with. They are bound to be watching you and every other member of the syndicate who's in New York. While we have been building our empire, Dewey has set up a massive operation to bring us down. That is all he exists to do—destroy everything we have worked hard to create."

"What if I were to intercede on your behalf with a member of the jury?"

Luciano's eyes darted left and right, then he ducked down even lower in his seat, before whispering, "Don't talk like that in front of me, Alex. You can't trust anyone nowadays—Dewey has his hooks into too many people."

"But it is possible."

"Anything can be done—the question is whether it will achieve the required outcome."

"What do you mean, Charlie?"

"Of course, I do not want you to tamper with the jury." Then in a lower voice, "If you bribe one member then that's just something else Dewey will hit you with when he arrests you. My informant tells me they intend to guard the jury members day and night so you wouldn't be able to get near to any one of them, even if you wanted to. This isn't Dutch's tax trial—this is much more serious. Dewey will use me to send a warning across the syndicate. I'm too high profile for him not to take me down."

"What do you want me to do?"

"You've done enough. Your investment capital makes sure Mendy is kept in new suits and either way, I'll go down fighting."

Alex considered Charlie's comments and wondered how to explain the difference between the bold words and his physical presence. The Italian was a deflated man, limbs limp by his side, face gaunt—the pocks on his cheeks almost appearing to want to leave his skin. Luciano talked a good talk but the threat of this trial was draining his life force away before Alex's eyes.

HE VISITED CHARLIE the following day, but this time the venue was his penthouse. Alex always felt at home here. Charlie had spent his money wisely on comfortable furniture and pleasant surroundings. Also, he'd been to the place so many times, there was nothing unusual about anything to do with the suite. Then a stranger walked into the room, causing Alex's eyebrows to rise.

"This is Arianna. I sent my family away to Florida, so they didn't have to run the gauntlet of the press hounds and I can concentrate on the work I have to do."

The explanation fell short of giving Alex a clue what Arianna's role was until she sat down next to Charlie and draped an arm around his neck while he leaned forward. He shrugged her off, grabbed a bunch of notes from his wallet and instructed her to go to Fifth Avenue and buy something nice. She grinned and didn't need to be told twice to skedaddle. When she was out the door, the men began their conversation.

"Back so soon, Alex. You must like my company."

"You know I do, Charlie, but that's not the main reason why I'm here."

The Italian sat on his couch and crossed his legs, a sign of how relaxed he was this morning compared to yesterday, but also it was the pose he adopted when it was time to talk business.

"I've been thinking about our arrangement regarding your heroin interests. Have you given much thought to what will happen if the worst comes to the worst?"

"If someone whacks me?"

"No, if Dewey convinces twelve men you are guilty of offering women to men who want to pay to sleep with them."

"I'm trying not to fill my head with those kinds of ideas. That's a loser's strategy."

"I understand, but, you shouldn't be caught off guard. Meyer is the cautious fella who must have spoken to you about planning for the unthinkable."

"You two been talking behind my back?"

"No, funnily enough I haven't seen him for two months. I have been looking at ways to prepare for my own future and the bigger stake I have in the heroin trade."

"What have you come up with, Alex?"

Now it was Alex's turn to sink back into his armchair and ready himself for his pitch to the most powerful gangster in America, the man who refused to call himself the boss of bosses.

"If Dewey gets his way, you must control your various interests while you're doing time."

"That's right."

"And you'll probably want fellas you can trust."

"That I would, Alex."

"So if you'd like to bear me in mind for the narcotics trafficking, that'd be mighty fine of you."

Charlie chuckled and Alex squirmed. This was as close as he would get to asking Luciano for a piece of the national heroin trade as he could utter. Every other time he'd got to enhance his empire thanks to one of the syndicate members, he had been offered and hadn't needed to ask.

"Sorry, Alex, but I can't help myself. Over the last month, countless guys have come to me offering to support me by taking my business from me before the gavel has even been struck and my sentence pronounced. You are the first fella to offer to borrow heroin trafficking and to give it back later."

Alex cleared his throat.

"What's yours is yours, Charlie. What else was I going to suggest?"

"Fellas like Albert Anastasia see my imminent jail time as an opportunity to seize what they do not have but want."

"We live together, we work together, Charlie."

"I agree, but not everyone sees things our way."

The two men fell quiet as they mulled over the conversation for a minute until Alex broke the silence.

"So have you figured out what you will do if Dewey gets his wish?"

"You, Meyer and Benny are my closest friends. We have been together off and on for as long as I can remember. I can't think of any bunch of fellas I trust more in this world and I will look to the three of you to run things on my behalf while I am away—if I am away."

"Thank you, Charlie."

"Don't mention it. You guys'll work hard to keep all the operations alive if I go down, but hopefully Mendy can weave a magic spell and save me from a lengthy stay at Sing Sing."

28

ALEX RECKONED SOMETHING was wrong the minute he hit the sidewalk outside his apartment. Ezra and Massimo had beckoned him out of the entrance and as he looked up and down, he noticed three men two hundred feet away just hanging around.

Nothing unusual in that, apart from their identical haircuts and impeccably polished shoes—the hallmark of a cop. One on his own would have been a coincidence because detectives hang out on street corners too. Two together wasn't a good sign but, again, they can be out to get donuts. Three was a team aiming to follow someone around the city, taking turns as the point man.

His lieutenants didn't seem to notice and opened the door to his vehicle. Alex tested out his theory and shook his head. "I'll walk the first few blocks—I need to clear my thoughts," he explained and Ezra hopped behind the wheel to slow-follow him, while Massimo hovered four paces back.

"Give me some space, Massimo. I'm going to pound the pavement and I don't want you scuffling at my heels."

Massimo remained silent but his eyes scrunched up in a quizzical expression—something was up.

Alex belted along the street until he reached the first corner and swiftly swung right and ducked into a storefront. Ten seconds later, Massimo walked past, barely shifting his head to acknowledge his boss and carried on half a block until he felt the overwhelming need to stop and tie a shoelace.

Thirty seconds more and a flatfoot hurried by, pretending to scratch his neck at the moment he passed Alex to force himself to turn his head in Alex's direction. Cheap theatricals—Ida could have done better.

He waited and shifted over one store to give the impression he was idly walking along and some items had caught his attention. Almost exactly on cue, if he had been counting, another gumshoe went past him thirty seconds later. At least Alex wasn't paranoid— these guys were following him for certain. He considered doubling back on them just to cause confusion, but that would have meant he'd signal to them he was onto them.

Instead, he resumed his journey at a slightly faster pace to force the cops up ahead to change gear and scatter, while the third unseen detective would need to jog to keep up.

Two blocks later and the cat-and-mouse game progressed with the detectives finally able to let Alex pass by, waiting near street corners so he wouldn't notice the same guys on the streets repeatedly showing up.

Alex switched left at the next corner and the gumshoes continued to keep up, while Massimo tailed him from only two hundred feet— following his orders to the letter. Ezra had given up running curbside and he parked on the same side as Alex, waited until he was at the end of a block and caught up.

At this point, Alex decided to lose the cops—he'd grown tired of this game and now he was just toying with them. Besides, he had some business to attend to which shouldn't be conducted in front of the prying eyes of law enforcement officials. He waited for Ezra's car to get to him and bent down to lean into the window.

"Any traffic we should know about?"

"None I've seen. You expecting company?"

"No questions, Ezra. When I jump into the back, I want you to hit the gas as fast as you can in one direction for at least fifteen blocks. Afterwards make a turn, I don't care where. Got it?"

Ezra nodded and followed his instructions as soon as Alex slammed the door shut. The car screeched forwards and Alex twisted his head to watch what was happening behind him. He saw Massimo stand still and at least two of the cops lurched forward for no good reason.

For the duration of their straight stretch, Alex kept checking all the lanes to the rear to make sure they hadn't missed any tail. By the time Ezra took a right, Alex was certain he could get to his meet with Meyer without hindrance.

Once he'd secured the financing he needed, he took an early lunch at Lindy's where he sat in his usual booth. Less than five minutes later, Alex gave his order for coffee and a pastrami on rye. He lit a cigarette and a clean-shaven suit, placed himself in the seat opposite and removed his hat, dangling it on the corner of his chair.

"Do you know who I am?"

"I read the newspapers, although you are uglier up close than on the front page, Thomas Dewey."

"Alex Cohen, do not make the mistake of treating me like a fool—and don't believe that you will escape my clutches like Dutch Schultz."

ALEX STARED THROUGH his eyes and into Dewey's soul to see the man intent on his downfall and that of his friends—because he'd sworn to uphold the law and did that to the best of his ability.

"Can I offer you a coffee or a cookie?"

"I won't take a single thing from you, Cohen, until I get the satisfaction of seeing you behind bars."

"Dewey, if you had anything on me, we wouldn't be having this conversation in Lindy's as you'd have dragged me over to some precinct and slammed me in cuffs. Sorry, threaten me a little less, tell me what you feel you need to say, and leave."

Dewey's cheeks tinged crimson but he continued.

"I want you to know that the grand jury investigating your tax affairs will reach its verdict soon and it's not looking good for you. If you have any sense, you'd spend less time eating pastrami and more time with a lawyer. You will need one."

"Thanks for the legal advice—where should I send my payment: to the Police Benevolence Fund?"

"Are you trying to bribe an officer of the law?"

"Dewey, you think too much of yourself. What makes you believe you are worth spending gelt on? To me, you are just another Fed with a badge and a desire to drag down hard-working guys who have made some money over the years. Your words make you sound like a Democrat, but the suits you wear shriek pure Republican."

"You'd know all about Tammany, wouldn't you, Cohen?"

"If you were right, my politician buddies who live in my back pocket would have hauled you off my case months ago. They haven't because they don't exist. I am just a guy who works for a living and earns some gelt to get by."

"It's your money the grand jury has been focused on. How you get it and what you report."

"I'm no Capone."

"The only difference between you and that Chicago shyster is that you are walking free—for the moment."

Alex ground his molars at the flippant way Dewey spoke about his friend—not that he'd seen or spoken with him since his last visit to the Windy City just before Alfonse was dragged down to the cells. He sighed and chewed on another bite of his sandwich.

"Dewey, were you bullied when you were a child?"

The special prosecutor moved his back in reaction to this pivot in the conversation.

"What do you mean, Cohen?"

"As a kid—did the other children in your class wait until you'd got past the school gate on your way home and push you and shove at you and knock you over? Later when you were in high school, if you were lucky enough to get a girl, would she choose the captain of the football team over you because he was more attractive than you?"

"Well, really."

"No, I'm sorry, I've got it all wrong, haven't I? You were the football captain and every girl flocked round you like flies to a shit heap."

"Cohen, I was team captain, but that is none of your business and has nothing to do with the predicament you are in now."

"You should get your story straight. I thought the grand jury's verdict hadn't come in yet. Today, I've got nothing to worry about apart from strangers interrupting my lunch. That's the trouble with New York—you are never more than six feet away from vermin."

Alex stared at Dewey again, his eyelids narrowing his eyes as he looked through the cop, whose cheeks were redder than before. He reached inside his jacket and Alex instinctively reached for his piece, hidden in his pants. Dewey froze, his hand still in plain sight.

"Cohen, I am about to reach in my jacket to give you my business card, should you want to talk. Judging by your stance, you might be carrying a concealed weapon. If I saw it, you'd be in the back of a meat wagon by now."

Dewey pulled the card out and threw it on the table, causing it to spin a half turn before landing by Alex's coffee cup. Then he stood up and took off. Ten minutes after Dewey departed, Alex left Lindy's to pay a visit to Mendy Greenberg and hire him as his lawyer.

29

WITH DEWEY NEVER far from the forefront of his mind, Alex continued to run Charlie's heroin supply operation into Brooklyn, as well as East Harlem with Buchalter and Anastasia. He also had his own territory running from the Bowery up to Midtown in which to sell those folded pieces of paper containing brown powder and an intense feeling of ecstasy.

An investment of three thousand dollars bought him a sack of processed heroin from overseas. This was more than the average criminal might earn in over a year of stick-ups in some hick town. But this was the Five Boroughs and Alex was a member of the syndicate, so the sacks were taken to one of the many warehouses they still owned from days spent bootlegging and was cut up with other powder to generate hundreds of hits, each carefully placed inside a piece of paper and folded twice. After, it was distributed to crews who stood on street corners and sold the narcotics at competitive rates.

There were many potential weaknesses in this chain of events—the arrival of the heroin by boat, its storage in the warehouses, the cutting up of the narcotic into sellable units and the transportation of the hits onto the street. This was a complex set of tasks and needed careful management, but the sack that cost Alex a few thousand netted close to half a million retail.

Charlie had the smarts to see the potential for this business when heroin was still legal back in the early twenties, but he had watched and waited and seized the moment when it finally appeared. He was a great checkers player.

A week after Dewey had interrupted Alex's lunch, Ezra called him from a warehouse in Brownsville.

"The last shipment hasn't arrived and I have men sitting around with nothing to do. Massimo said there was some kind of delay. I can't get hold of him and I'm hoping you know what's happening."

"I thought this had all been taken care of. Charlie's contact in Palermo sent me a telegram to say the boat sailed two days late, but they expected to make up the time on the journey."

"No such luck, Alex. It's way overdue and I have no idea what's going on."

"Leave it with me, Ezra. Send your boys home on a full day's pay. Let's keep them sweet today, at any rate."

A QUICK TRIP to Massimo's and the explanation was simple.

"The ship vanished."

"What do you mean, Massimo?"

"You heard me—straight up. There was radio communication with the boat three days ago. It met strong winds during its crossing so hadn't made up any time that was lost with the troubles in Sicily."

"And?"

"Nothing. Zilch. It's like God picked up the vessel and took it we don't know where."

"This will be no divine hand, Massimo. Someone got to the ship before it could land. Accidents do not happen to shipments worth six figure sums."

"Who?"

"That I can't say, but either the captain joined somebody else's payroll, or the boat was hijacked. Neither is good for us because it means we are down one boatload of heroin."

Massimo gulped as he imagined his profit floating out of the window in his apartment where they sat.

"If it wasn't the gods, whose hand was it?"

"Massimo, that is an excellent question and I need to identify the person as soon as possible. Tell your crews to sniff around and find out. Before the end of the day, I want the name of the person who stole my heroin."

As the sun vanished behind the skyline, Massimo phoned Alex at his apartment.

"I have the answer to your question."

"Good. Who?"

"Anastasia. He issued the order and my men tell me he has already unloaded the ship and is processing it with his people. By tomorrow the first consignment will reach the streets."

Alex let out a lengthy breath. If it had been some young Turk, he would have been able to handle the situation himself—a little local difficulty requiring a visit from his lieutenants, a dose of retribution and the return of his property. That this had been sponsored by Albert Anastasia created considerably more complications and meant everything was a lot more dangerous—when a made man muscles into your turf, there can only be trouble ahead.

"SO, WHAT I'M asking is if you'd have any issues if Albert met with an accident?"

Meyer, Benny, and Alex were sitting in Meyer's suite at the Benjamin Hotel on Fiftieth having a conversation instigated by Alex. It had been twenty-four hours since Anastasia had stolen the heroin, and Alex was the only person who seemed the least bit perturbed—and that was making him angry.

Benny rotated his hat around a stretched-out finger, as was his habit during these meetings, and sniggered at Alex's question. Both Meyer and Alex scowled at him, but for different reasons. Meyer loved Benny like he was a brother, although a sibling who didn't take matters seriously enough for his liking. Alex just did not appreciate being laughed at by Siegel.

"And what is the likelihood of Albert being knocked down by a passing car, Alex?"

"Much higher than two days ago, Meyer."

The fedora continued to twirl and Benny said nothing—choosing to concentrate on the rotating headgear instead.

"I have proof he has stolen half a million of my assets and that needs to be resolved."

"What assets?"

"Uncut heroin, Meyer."

"And what is the evidence?"

"A missing ship, Anastasia's men crammed into a processing plant. His guys hitting my streets with my heroin and not paying me a dime."

Meyer crossed his legs and picked a piece of fluff off his knee, flicking it onto the ground. His expression showed he was mulling over what Alex had said. Given the scale of the deal, this was a serious matter despite the whimsy Benny saw in everything.

"Alex, how do you know that a third party didn't steal the ship and merely passed on the goods to Albert?"

"I cannot be certain—not like in a court of law—but who are you suggesting had the capability to steal a boat in the middle of the Atlantic Ocean and transport the narcotic ashore and shift it into Anastasia's warehouse? The only people I can think of in this city are sat in this room."

"Or Charlie."

"What Benny?"

"Charlie has the muscle for this."

Alex exhaled loudly.

"It was Charlie's dope in the first place, Benny. Why would he steal his own heroin from himself? You're not making any sense, man."

"Just saying, that's all."

"If you have nothing positive to contribute, perhaps it would be better for you to remain silent, Benny."

"All right, Meyer. Only trying to help."

Alex and Meyer eyed each other in exasperation—Benny was acting more strangely than normal, and neither understood why. He did this now and again—it was one of the reasons he worked alone because of his difficult behavior when mixing with people, even his friends.

"Back to the situation at hand, Alex. How certain are you that Albert is behind this?"

"As sure as I can be. If you are asking me if I saw him instruct his men to take over the boat then no, I didn't."

"That's what I thought, Alex."

"But, Meyer, despite Benny's sense of humor, he has a point. The only other person who'd have the resources to do this would be Charlie and as that's not possible, we are left with Albert Anastasia."

"This is circumstantial evidence, Alex. You can't tell the difference between Albert carrying out this deed or someone from Philadelphia or Chicago coming over here, pushing their way into our business and then selling the heroin on to your Murder Corporation partner."

"Are you telling me you really believe that's what's happened, Meyer?"

"Of course not, but it doesn't matter what I think. Do you reckon you can convince the others you are right?"

"Meyer, that is not what I am asking. I want to know how you two feel about this. If you aren't behind me then there's no point calling a syndicate meeting because I would lose the vote—when your friends don't believe you then others are unlikely to side with you either."

"There's no need to be like that, Alex. I just know we have to be watertight before the syndicate will agree to a hit on a made man."

"Then I'll get the proof you require, because Albert is trying to destroy my world."

30

NOT FOR THE first time in his life, Alex stood in an empty warehouse with Ezra and Massimo for company. There was another guy in the place, but he had his wrists and ankles tied and muslin stuffed into his mouth. Willis Tanzi wasn't going anywhere for a while.

Alex paced around—when he reached one wall, he turned and pounded the floor until he got to the other side. Meanwhile, Massimo stood next to Tanzi while Ezra sat opposite him, staring him down. Beads of sweat had formed on Tanzi's forehead and breathing was far from easy, judging by the snorting sounds squeezing out of his nostrils.

The three fellas talked loudly over the snorts and acted as though Tanzi wasn't sat in front of them, bruises forming around his cheeks where the lieutenants had slapped him about long enough for him to understand the seriousness of his situation. Alex began the interrogation with a calm voice and relaxed posture.

"Willis, do you know why you are here?"

A shake of his head and Tanzi's breathing increased a notch.

"You were overheard discussing a matter close to my heart. Have you any idea what that might be?"

Another snort, another shake of the head. Several of the beads of sweat flew from their resting place on his forehead and landed like miniature salty raindrops onto the floor.

"You are here because of a shipment which never made it to port."

Eyes widened as Tanzi realized what was going on. He shook his head repeatedly as if to emphasize what little information he had to offer.

"Would you be so kind as to take that cloth out of his mouth? Willis appears to want to tell us something."

Alex looked at Ezra when he said this, but Massimo was the one to carry out the instruction. His friend remained sat, staring at Tanzi with pure menace. Massimo threw the rag onto the floor and Tanzi choked for a minute, pleased to be released from the suffocating taste of the material jammed to within spit of his tonsils. Alex raised a hand and pointed to a spot beyond where Tanzi could see.

Massimo sauntered over and returned with an open bottle of beer, which he gingerly put against the man's lips to let him take two sips —just enough to moisten his mouth and the back of his throat. Then Massimo walked away again with the bottle, out of Tanzi's line of sight.

"I don't know nothing. You gotta believe me."

"Willis, you are wrong, my friend. First, you spoke loudly in a bar about how you had been on board a ship at precisely the time when my vessel was being snatched from me. Second, I do not trust a word that comes out of your mouth—part of your job is to convince me you speak the truth. So please don't tell me you are innocent and haven't been involved in the robbery, because everybody in this room knows you have."

Tanzi swung his head round right then left, to catch sight of the three men's location. Massimo had positioned himself in the guy's blind spot.

"Sorry. Yes. Sure. I was in the crew on the tugboat that grabbed your shipment, but I was only operating under orders."

"Willis, I know you are not the mastermind behind this scheme— don't worry about that."

Tanzi's shoulders wilted slightly as though some weight had been lifted from his torso. Alex's voice stayed softly spoken and he ensured his body remained as relaxed as he could make it to keep Tanzi at his ease.

"So tell me, what were the orders you were instructed to follow—if you were the monkey and not the organ grinder?"

"Just to sail the tug out to meet the boat, climb aboard and get the captain to take it to the shore where trucks would be waiting."

"What were you instructed to do with my men?"

"No one said to do anything, but we knew what was expected of us."

"And what was that, Willis?"

Tanzi glanced at Ezra and turned his attention back to Alex.

"There were to be no survivors. Once we had unloaded the cargo, we were to scuttle the ship. Either we shot them when we boarded or they drowned."

Alex ground his molars and breathed through his nose for twenty seconds until the wall of anger within him had subsided enough to speak again.

"Thank you for your honesty, Willis. Lesser men would have spun a story, but you have spared yourself the embarrassment of untruths."

"I figure the only chance I have is to be straight up with you guys. If you detect a lie on my lips, then you'll torture me, then kill me and I really don't want that to happen."

"I reckon you do not—and I would much rather find out what I need without asking either of my friends here to do you harm. Violence has no place in business. It stops men thinking clearly—they panic and tell you what they think you want to be told. To prevent that, you must cause them immense pain and that takes time and effort."

Tanzi blinked the sweat out of his eyelashes and absorbed the underlying threat behind Alex's statement. His panting increased and Alex waited for the man to wade through the panic attack. This was difficult—he needed the guy to be fearful enough to respond but not so scared that he'd admit to killing Abraham Lincoln.

"So can you tell me who issued the orders you followed?"

"I don't know."

"Willis, you disappoint me. I would have been sure you'd remember the name of the person who instructed what to do and when. Surely, that's something hard to forget, especially when you've been hustled off the street with a sack over your head and taken into this warehouse for a conversation with me."

"No one told me anything."

"Now that is a lie, Willis, because you said earlier that you were following orders. Who gave them to you?"

An edge had entered Alex's voice and he leaned forward two inches in his seat. Not sufficient to appear menacing, but enough of a change to imply that worse was to come if Tanzi didn't toe the line.

"My friend Paulie told me the scoop—I wasn't in the room when it happened."

"Who is this Paulie? Do we need to bring him in here?"

"Jeez, no. He has a wife and a family."

"So do I, Willis, but if I had received instructions like your pal Paulie, I'd expect to be hauled into this warehouse to explain my actions."

"He heard it from another guy. You know how these things work. Nobody knows anything and that way the bosses stay safe."

"Willis, unless you tell me something more useful, you will force me to invite Paulie to join us and he has a wife and kids, you say, which means he is far more likely to spill what he has than you appear to be."

"I… All I know is that this kind of operation wasn't cheap and paid very well. They needed guys who would keep their cool when the going got rough and were professional, y'know?"

"And that means Paulie won't talk?"

"He knows about as much as I do. And I'm sure of that because we talked about it, him and me. We wanted to know who was paying our wages. It's only natural."

Massimo shifted his weight behind Tanzi, although the guy had no way of knowing that had happened. The glass bottle slipped out of the lieutenant's fingers and landed on the floor with a smash of glass, causing Tanzi to visibly jump.

"Just the beer—fell out of his hand. An accident, Willis. Don't worry about it. Go on."

"Yeah, like I was saying, we didn't know who was running the gig, but we got an idea who was backing it."

"What do you mean?"

"The money man. I told you it was an expensive operation and word was that Buchalter was funding it."

"Louis Buchalter?"

"That's what I said. Louis was the financier."

"Thank you, Willis, you have been most helpful."

Alex signaled a motion with his hand again and Ezra continued to stare at Tanzi, only this time the corners of his lips moved upwards. Meanwhile, Massimo stepped forward and grabbed Tanzi by the chin, whipping his head back. Holding the neck of the beer bottle in the other hand, he swiped across Willis Tanzi's throat with the naked shard of glass, sharp as a blade. Sliced him from ear to ear and let him droop down, blood spurting out of his throat like a kosher chicken in its death throes.

"Throw this one into the Hudson and then pay a call on Paulie. Find out if he knows anything of any use and kill him too. Chances are Tanzi told us the truth."

31

FOR THE NEXT three nights, Alex woke at four and couldn't get back to sleep. The following evening he walked the streets of Hoboken after he spent the evening hiding in plain sight. If nothing else, he figured Dewey's men wouldn't be able to follow him out of the state—they followed all the rules.

Then he paid a nafka to spend the night with him hoping their exploits would be enough to tire him out and make him snore through until morning, but no dice. She was merely a warm body to curl up next to as he had no interest in doing anything sexual with her, despite the girl's beauty and his hope that this would save him from himself.

By the end of the week, Alex didn't know which way to turn. There was now a heroin supply drought in New York—no matter how hard he tried, there was no source to buy from in the city or along the entire Eastern Seaboard. No one would trade with him and they wouldn't say why.

To make matters worse, every time he stepped out onto a sidewalk, Alex was being surveilled by the cops. The only good thing was that he wasn't paranoid, but that didn't decrease the stress of the situation at all for him.

Alex stayed away from Charlie until Friday—at this point he hadn't slept a wink the last two nights at all. He had held back because he knew that the pandering trial started on Monday and he had been trying not to bother his friend so close to the beginning of his day in court.

"THANKS FOR SEEING me, Charlie."

"Always a pleasure to break bread with a friend such as you, Alex."

Charlie had chosen Lindy's as the venue for their rendezvous mainly out of nostalgia and because he couldn't be sure he'd be able to take a trip to the restaurant again in the near future. Alex reckoned this was the reason but didn't want to ask—he had no desire to remind Charlie of how likely he was to face prison time under Dewey's prosecution.

"Are you still certain you don't need me to have a conversation with a jury member?

"Alex, you are very kind but my answer remains no. If Mendy can't get me off, then there is no point crippling a juror—Dewey will only come back smelling more blood and want to find out who nobbled his jury."

"You are not the only one to be at the wrong end of his sights. His guys have been tailing me for weeks."

"And you brought them here?"

"No, Charlie. Whenever I have any actual business to do, I ditch them. You should know me better than that. Although, there is nothing criminal about two men eating lunch together."

"True, but you did just offer to tamper with a jury which is a federal crime, Alex."

Alex laughed. "You can't prove nothing, cop." Then it was Charlie's turn to grin and they settled into their food. By the time they finished their meal, Alex was feeling relaxed, if tired.

"These have been some fabulous years, Charlie, wouldn't you say?"

"Sure have and it's not over yet. Don't forget that."

"I appreciate this isn't the greatest time, Charlie, but I need to ask a favor of you."

"Tell me and I'll do my best to help."

Alex stirred the spoon in his coffee for too long before responding because he wasn't sure of Charlie's reply.

"Albert and Louis are closing in on the dope trade—with you keeping your eye on Dewey, they have attacked our heroin transportation into the country. They've stolen the latest cargo from Sicily and there is nothing I can do."

"What do you want from me?"

"Authorize a hit on Anastasia. Let me whack the guy—Buchalter is only supplying the gelt—nothing more.

CHARLIE SMILED, LICKED the pad of his first finger and picked off the last crumb of cheesecake from his plate. A sip of coffee and he replaced the cup on its saucer.

"Alex, you never cease to amaze me. What went down between you and Albert to make you want him dead so much?"

"Nothing happened—he's been trying to cut into our rackets for a long time. I have tried to contain the problem and not bother you with it, but now your interests are aligned with mine and I'm hoping you will see what needs to be done. And soon, before we lose any more money or worsen our reputation."

"From the moment I introduced you to Albert and Louis at the first syndicate meeting, I could tell from the way you stood that you were not comfortable with them. This request of yours has nothing to do with whether you get on as people—it has to be tied to business."

"Charlie, this isn't anything personal—it is all business. He has attacked our drug supply line into New York. He has stolen our ship, taken our heroin and killed our men. This is business."

"And do you have proof for this allegation?"

"Suddenly everyone's a lawyer. No, I don't have witnesses who heard Anastasia issue the order, but there is a smoking gun—we have no heroin to sell and his boys are hitting our streets and selling the only powder available in the city. And I had a guy admit he was in the crew that assailed the boat."

"That's not enough, Alex, and you know it, otherwise you'd have put the proposal to the syndicate."

"I'm not asking the syndicate—it's you, Charlie."

"There are two problems—even if I wanted to help, my hands are tied. Albert is a made man—and that means I can't touch him, you can't touch him. No one can without permission from Sicily—and you won't get that as a Jew in New York. No disrespect, but that is the way the old-timers think. It is almost at the point when they only talk to guys born on the island. Everyone else they judge as an outsider."

"That's ridiculous."

"It is the reality of the situation. Like I say, it isn't down to me. I will not touch a hair on the head of a boss without approval."

"Would you ask on my behalf then. You're Sicilian, aren't you?"

"I am, but that is only half the issue. I said there were two difficulties and the old country dons are one thing. The other is that I'm not sure you have enough to make your allegation stick."

"But..." Charlie raised a finger to stop Alex in his tracks.

"I understand you spoke with a guy who'd stolen your boat and the most he gave up which was certain was that Louis had been the money behind the deal. Your man only heard rumors after that."

"Sure, but there was another..."

"Let me finish, Alex. There was indeed another of the gang, but when Massimo interrogated him, you got bupkis. Like every good gang member, he refused to give up a name. There is a vow of omertà for a reason."

"So you won't help me then."

"Less of the won't and more of the can't. Show me something concrete and I'll put the word out in a flash, but right now you've got nothing to hang your hat on—and do not misunderstand me; I would happily take Anastasia out because I also don't like the way he conducts his business."

They continued in silence for a minute while they both finished their coffees. When the waiter asked if they wanted anything else, they both declined and Alex ensured he was the one who paid for what they both feared might be Charlie's last lunch in Lindy's for quite some time. When they left, they shook hands and hugged, Alex patting Charlie repeatedly on the back as if to show how much he cared for his friend through the act of slapping him firmly. Charlie mirrored the gesture and then they separated on the sidewalk and Alex walked briskly away.

32

TO SAY THAT Alex was dissatisfied with his time with Charlie was an understatement. The disquiet idled in his gut all afternoon so that by the evening, he yearned for some company he could rely on and to sleep at night again. In the absence of any other ideas, he made his way over to Ida, up through the service elevator and into her suite.

"Darling, how fabulous to see you again. Come through, you have arrived just in time to mix me a martini."

He nodded, threw his jacket onto an empty chair, undid his tie, and sauntered over to the drinks trolley and whipped out the cocktail shaker in the shape of a penguin—Ida liked to add quirky touches to her surroundings.

Meanwhile, she languished on her chaise longue, allowing the split in her ankle-length skirt to reveal the side of her leg above her knee. Alex couldn't decide if she was being coquettish or just careless in how she sat. The woman's mind was addled by the narcotics she'd been inhaling the past two decades and she behaved erratically at times.

Alex walked over with a pair of wide-brimmed glasses and passed one to Ida, who took it graciously in a long-fingered hand and clinked the sides before taking a long sip.

"Marvelous. You make a fabulous martini, darling."

"You're welcome. How have you been?"

She started by regaling him with a meandering tale of woe that commenced with her adventure in the elevator the day before and pursued a trajectory that Alex found hard to follow. To take his mind off her prattling, he absentmindedly stroked the stretch of her leg which had become visible when she sat down.

His beau continued her story as he played with her knee, occasionally taking another mouthful of her cocktail, but not seeming to stop until the narrative and her glass had run dry. She held out the receptacle and Alex collected it from her, poured two more glasses from the shaker and returned to where he had been sitting.

For the first time in a week, Alex relaxed—as though Ida's prattling was a soothing tonic that blotted out the callings from the rest of the world invading his head. A hunger in the pit of his stomach bore inside of him in a way he had not experienced for more years than he cared to remember.

By the late afternoon, Ida wanted a fix, so she took out her pipe and Alex consumed another martini while she was flaked out. He made sure he remained focused only on what was going on inside the room. Maybe it was the effect of the opium smoke floating in the atmosphere or maybe he was just plain tired, but either way, when she roused herself, he grabbed her by the hand and led her into the bedroom.

WHEN ALEX WOKE up a few hours later, Ida was stroking his chest—the reason he'd regained consciousness, perhaps. He placed his palm on hers to stop the motion of her fingers.

"Thanks for being here for me."

"I had no plans for today anyway, darling."

"No, Ida, I meant over the years."

"You really are too kind. I am the one who should thank you—I live in this marvelous hotel suite because you are precious enough to pay for it. You buy me pretty things and cover the lodging fees every month. Few guys would have done that for a girl like me."

"The gravy train might come into the station fairly soon."

"What do you mean, Alex?"

"There are several men who are coming after me and I don't know how long I can fend them all off."

"I have every faith that good will prevail."

"Ida, one of the men is a prosecutor. He won't stop until he has me in chains."

"Then, darling, get rid of the tiresome fellow. You might not talk to me about your business, but I read the newspapers. If half of what is printed is true, then you know what you must do."

"Don't think I haven't considered whacking Dewey," Ida's eyes opened wider, reflecting that she didn't have a clue which cop Alex had been referring to. "But nobody'll support me. They're all turning their backs on me."

"If you deal with this ruffian, will you be able to resolve the other matters more easily?"

"With Dewey gone, the rest of the fellas would be so transfixed in fear, I could take care of other matters with no one able to stop me."

"There's the solution to your problems then. You and I should talk business more often."

Alex smiled and put his hands behind his head while Ida planted kisses all over his body until he lapsed back into unconsciousness.

ALEX OPENED HIS eyes again to find himself in Ida's bed—he had slept like a baby all night long. Bliss. She had rolled over and taken all the sheets, leaving him cold and naked, so he got up, grabbed his shorts, and padded over to the kitchen to make a coffee. Still Ida didn't stir.

He sat in an easy chair overlooking the bed and lit a smoke, cupping his drink in one hand and flicking the ash off the end of his cigarette with the other. The chink of light through the curtains landed on Ida's feet, which were poking out from the bottom of the sheets.

The tranquility of this moment soaked through him and Alex allowed himself the luxury of staring at Ida, drinking and smoking. As he put the cup down on a nearby side table, Ida awoke, turned over to see him better and smiled. She raised an arm for Alex to bring over a lit cigarette for her. He clambered over her body to lie next to her, inhaling her warm scent and enjoying the calm they inhabited.

"So will you kill him then?"

The question seemed to come from nowhere and Alex recoiled from Ida just on hearing the words.

"What are you talking about?"

"Dewey, darling. Are you going to do him in?"

The ceiling spun around him and Alex was glad he was lying down, otherwise he would have surely found himself sprawled on the ground. He blinked hard and tried to breathe normally despite the pounding in his chest. An acid taste burst into his mouth and Alex realized he had to stop this from happening. He hadn't been thinking straight when he shared what he was considering with her the night before.

He sat up and rolled on top of Ida with a smile on his face and a gentle touch to her cheek. One knee either side of her torso, Alex grabbed both her wrists, pulling them above her head. Ida glanced at both hands, a flash of concern on her face, while Alex bent down and planted a long kiss on her lips.

"I never wanted to leave you," he whispered as he leaned back slightly and moved one wrist to his other hand so he grasped both arms in a palm, freeing up the other hand to grab at the pillow behind her head. Before Ida knew what was going on, Alex had ripped the pillow out from under her and placed it over her face and mouth.

She tried to clutch at the pillow, but he held onto her wrists like a vice. Besides, he had her pinned down with the weight of his body so there wasn't much she could do. Ida only took two minutes to stop struggling and for her arms to go limp. Alex waited another thirty seconds just in case and eased the pressure off the pillow, but nothing.

He got off her and stood on the floor to survey the scene. Alex replaced the pillow under her head, threw the sheets over her body and maneuvered Ida's limbs so you could be forgiven for thinking she had died in her sleep.

Then he picked out his cigarette butts from the ashtrays scattered around the suite and cleaned his martini glass and coffee cup. With no obvious trace of his existence in the room that night, Alex put on his clothes and left the building using the service elevator.

While he might not have wanted to end things that way, Alex knew he was never going to leave her because she was never going to be worth the effort of saying, "It's time we called it quits, babe."

33

A MEETING OF the syndicate took place, only without Charlie as he was otherwise engaged spending his first day in court on the pandering changes brought by Dewey. Everyone agreed how sorry they were that he was so indisposed, but they also noted that life must go on and agreed Johnny Torrio should chair the discussions in Charlie's place.

Torrio was a square-headed fella and a smart Italian who had come over to America when he was two and made his fortune through hard work and an unceasing use of his muscles. He might have taken a back seat in New York the last few years, but he was as much the brains behind the creation of the syndicate as Charlie. When he asked everybody to come to order, they did so as promptly as if Luciano had been in the room.

"Thank you everybody for coming today. I appreciate that we all lead busy lives and a day trip to Ithaca was not high on everyone's priority list."

Various nods and mumbling to denote agreement from the twenty men assembled around the boardroom table in the no-name hotel which had been selected for the meeting. The first few minutes were spent with each boss describing issues they were having with local and federal cops. Where appropriate, others chimed in with suggestions on how to join forces to resolve these difficulties.

Eventually, the lead returned to Torrio, who invited Buchalter to start the next item on the agenda.

"Thank you, Johnny. I stand here before you with a simple request. I want permission for us to hit Joe Rosen."

His statement was met with complete and utter silence. Louis looked around the room, trying to understand the response he was receiving. Torrio offered him a clue.

"Louis, explain who Rosen is, as most of us have not heard of him before."

"Sure, sorry. Rosen is a trucker in the garment industry."

"Schmatta. Now I know all about that," Benny interjected and chuckles rippled across the room from all the Jewish attendees. Louis waited for the ripple to die down and then he continued.

"The situation is very simple. I have asked Rosen to leave town and yet he remains in Brooklyn and refuses to depart."

"I'm not sure we should kill someone just for ignoring a polite request." Meyer made the comment with no hint of irony in his voice, even though he knew the polite request should have been more assertive than that.

"You seem to ignore the reason I sent him out of town in the first place, Meyer."

"Then describe it to us, Louis. You haven't explained yourself very well. I think I speak for everyone here when I say we are happy to condemn the man to death, if only we understood why he must die."

"Forgive me, Meyer. I seem to have started in the middle. Let me go back to the beginning and try again."

Meyer nodded consent and, judging by the response in the room, the others agreed—Alex clenched his jaw, not wanting to side with Buchalter given this man stood in front of the syndicate had financed the hijacking of his heroin shipment.

"Around six months ago, we muscled in on the National Garment Workers of America, a relatively peaceful union which had more money than its members needed. All was good in that we convinced the leadership to either step aside or take an income from us. Roll forward four months and the union was a regular money earner and we fomented the occasional murmur of disquiet to shake down the odd factory owner to increase revenues further. Some members were less enthusiastic with our presence and they either got on the bus or stood in front of it. Joe Rosen did not ride on the public transport."

"Socialist," Benny whispered, but this time he didn't get his desired response as the group had been hooked into Louis' story.

"I didn't make a big deal over this—inevitably, some people can't get used to change, especially when it turns up in suits, fedoras and with loaded guns. So Joe Rosen left the union and stopped hauling clothing for a living."

"Can you skip to the part why you need him dead, please, Louis?" Meyer was nervous how long this tale would take as he wanted to get back to Manhattan before nightfall—he had an appointment he did not want to miss.

"That is when Rosen talked with Thomas Dewey."

The name caused the room to erupt as people banged on the tables, shouted, and generally allowed their tempers to run high at the mere mention of the special prosecutor.

"LET ME GET this straight, Louis. You are telling us that this Rosen squealed to the cops."

Anastasia looked Buchalter square in the eye because the Italian operated under a simple policy—give nothing to the police even if they ask for the time of day.

"I reckon so."

"Believe or know? The difference is very important." Meyer had leaned in and taken his chin out of his hand.

"The guy lost his job because he wouldn't stay in the union. He visited Manhattan three times in one week. What else was the chump doing apart from spilling his guts to Dewey?"

"Perhaps he had a sick aunt at Mount Sinai."

Louis gave Benny a disdainful sideways glance and ignored him beyond that, even though he had generated a few smiles around the room.

"Did you have Rosen tailed? Do you know where he actually went in Manhattan?"

"Meyer, no I don't. He was one of a group of truckers who refused to pay their new union dues. We didn't mind because, as we all appreciate, when you take over a labor union, some old members leave. But it doesn't matter because you've still got everyone else putting up and shutting up. There's natural wastage."

"Then you are asking us to agree to a hit based on your belief that he's a rat? You don't know for sure."

"Meyer, I keep saying to you I can't offer you any hard evidence. All I am certain is that Rosen lost his job, before he left the union, and for a while afterwards, he complained to anybody who'd listen about how the union had gone to seed and that the likes of me were having undue influence, as he called it. The next thing you know he is going to Manhattan for entire days and not telling people where he'd been when he returned. Not even his wife knows what he's up to."

"In that case, it isn't an aunt he's visiting—it's a Midtown madam or a mistress."

"Benny, these asides really aren't helping." Torrio used a stage whisper so Benny understood he had received a public admonishment—his interventions were bordering on the childish.

"As I was saying, the only reason a person is secretive is because he has something to hide. Rosen is talking to the cops and it won't be about the intricacies of the Talmud."

"This is not meant to be the least bit flippant," Benny spoke, "but our problem isn't with Rosen but with Dewey. I understand this matter has come before this group before, but why don't we hit Dewey? We may or may not be sure that Rosen is a rat, but we know for certain that the special prosecutor needs to be taken down a peg or two. Let's deal with the bigger fish."

Torrio stepped in before anybody else could respond.

"Benny, your suggestion is not without merit as some in this room will no doubt agree, but as a point of order, right now we are addressing the question of whether Rosen should meet his maker sooner rather than later. After that, we can return to the problem of Thomas Dewey."

Siegel parted his lips as if he was about to say something, then thought better of it and shut his mouth and shrugged instead. Alex hoped the idea wouldn't get lost in this Rosen nonsense—Louis clearly didn't have sufficient proof to support his desire to see the guy dead, whereas Dewey needed to be taken care of.

Torrio continued to hold the floor.

"It seems to me that there are two issues with Rosen. First is that he appears to be squealing and second that people believe he is squealing and see that we are doing nothing about it. The first is subject to doubt, but the second point is an absolute certainty. Whatever happens, everybody must know that we will not tolerate dropping a dime to the cops. Who votes for the hit on Rosen to take place?"

Unanimous decision.

"That's agreed then. All I counsel is that we do not rush into the hit. Unless Louis receives any hard evidence, then I am happy for us to wait a month or two. When he drops to the sidewalk in a pool of blood, it will be more dramatic that we took our time and responded as cold as stone."

34

MENDY GREENBERG OCCUPIED a compact room in a midtown Park Avenue office block, so at least Alex knew the money he paid him wasn't wasted on swanky furniture and marble flooring. The level of discomfort you felt when you sat in one of his chairs emphasized the sense of disquiet many of his clients experienced as they discussed with him their battles with the law.

Some lawyers specialized in fighting injustice, operating on a no-win, no-fee basis to enable the downtrodden masses the opportunity to have their day in court and to get back at the man. Mendy's moral compass operated in a different direction—he preferred to represent those who generally were guilty before being presumed innocent, but still didn't want to go to jail or pay a fine.

For him, growing up in the Bowery was simply another way to build up trust with his clientele as he came from the same stink hole as they did, only he had studied at night until he got himself a certificate to practice law in the state of New York.

"So what are my chances, Mendy?"

"I'd say there are very strong odds that you will do time—unless Dewey drops dead, that is."

Alex stared at him and crossed his legs, resting both palms on his uppermost knee. He tilted his head slightly to one side before responding.

"Are you suggesting that if Dewey were to be six feet under then my problem would go away?"

"Even with client confidentiality, there is no way I would ever recommend that you commit a crime to reduce your prospects for hard time. The New York City Bar Association would take a very dim view of that suggestion without a shadow of a doubt."

"So you are advising me that if Dewey were dead, then my situation would improve but you are not telling me to do anything about it."

"Exactly. I knew you'd understand."

"And yet you think I will be in jail before the end of the year."

"Dewey's case is strong. My understanding is that they have a paper trail connecting you and your income to a variety of revenue streams and you haven't paid a dime in tax since you came to this country."

"I kept no documents—it was all in my head. It's only in the last few years that Charlie suggested I should have some paperwork to show the cops if they came snooping."

"Alex, I will not make any statements about the quality of the advice you received from another of my clients, especially one as powerful as Charlie. Suffice to say, you should have got a second opinion."

"What's done is done, though. From where I am now, you'd say I'm on a one-way ticket up the river?"

"Yep. The most we can hope for is a lenient judge so you don't get the maximum sentence."

"Which is?"

"You don't want to know—more years than Alfonse received."

"And what do you advise me to do?"

"These are your options—don't shoot the messenger but you asked me the question. First, proclaim your innocence but say nothing and take the full force of the law. Take the fifth on anything and everything they ask—that way, your friends will know that you looked after their interests and they will look after you when you go inside. Second, you cut a deal with Dewey. Plead guilty to the tax evasion charges. The difference with the first option is that you'll spend next to no time in court and the judge will give you a shorter sentence because we will negotiate the duration with Dewey. Third, we throw ourselves at the mercy of the court—go to trial and convince a jury you're innocent of all charges."

"Is that all I got?"

"Alex, I can pretend to you we have a watertight case and that as soon as I explain to the jury they'll roll over and play ball—but how you have no discernible legal income apart from working at a union for a year or two before the war and yet you own a string of establishments and real estate, as well as possessing enough money to afford your lavish lifestyle?"

"How about jury tampering?"

"Again, I cannot tell you in too strong a form how I am not suggesting you should do this. In your situation, I'd bear in mind that if a jury heard the evidence Dewey has against you and then voted not guilty, even a senile judge would have to demand a mistrial or get the cops to arrest the twelve of them. It is not a wise option, Alex."

"What would you do if you were in my shoes?"

"Alex, that's not for me to say. It is your decision as it's your life."

ALEX DIDN'T SLEEP for a minute that night and when he opened his newspaper which was delivered every morning to his door, he found a note hidden in between the pages so that none of his guys would see it. There was a time and an address—and it was signed Thomas Dewey.

His instincts told him to either take the first train to Florida or plain ignore it. Then Alex thought some more and realized that he would have to deal. Just because he didn't want Dewey on his back, the truth was the special prosecutor was clinging to his neck and would not go away. He put a call through to Mendy.

"I know I've asked this before, but with whom would you share what we discuss?"

"Nobody under ordinary circumstances."

"And what happens in extraordinary circumstances?"

"If you tell me you are about to commit a crime, then I am supposed to inform the police. I try not to have good hearing sometimes."

"What if something I plan to do will impact another of your clients?"

"Whatever you tell me, stays with me. I will not disclose to Charlie what we discuss—just as I do not inform you what Charlie and I say. That's no way to conduct business."

Alex maintained a silence on the line as he mulled this over. Mendy was right—with the people he had as clients, if the lawyer broke client privilege then he'd be dead within a week.

"I've been summoned to meet with Dewey this afternoon and I need you there."

"Do you know how you will respond when he offers you a deal?"

"Depends what's on the table. If I can avoid jail time, that'd be good."

"Alex, Dewey will want his photo on the front pages with you being led away in handcuffs."

"Then I'll take the smallest jail term that's on offer."

"Which means you'll be expected to admit to your criminal activities, lose your money and, dare I say it, most likely your friends shall walk away."

"Because I'll have to name them as protagonists in my business dealings?"

"Yes. While you have protected yourself relatively well over the years by not keeping any records, there are still going to be witnesses to conversations. The good news for you is that you have been very careful around syndicate members, but you will throw your lieutenants to the wolves."

"And we can't be certain that somebody didn't hear something over all these years."

"Exactly right. Don't forget that Dewey has a small army of cops who can spend months harassing people until they find a shred of evidence, because from that they build a case against any of your work associates."

"Can we not hem Dewey in? Make him keep to my tax affairs and not go stomping all over everybody else's business?"

"You wish. Look, Alex, if you cooperate over the tax evasion, you'll get a light sentence and pay a hefty fine. If you plead not guilty, then it'll be down to a jury to decide and Dewey has the proof to send you away for a very long time and strip you of all the money you have ever earned."

"If I cut a deal, I must leave the country. Everyone'll think I spilled my guts."

"They will only expect you sang like a canary if you walk down the streets humming."

ALEX TOLD EZRA and Massimo not to bother going with him as he had some private business to attend to and they shrugged and left him at the door of the Lexington Hotel on Forty-eighth Street where Alex had lived ever since Sarah walked out. He hopped in a taxi and went straight to the address on the piece of paper.

When he got out of the cab, Alex saw the rundown fleapit of a hotel that Dewey had chosen for their rendezvous. There was no one at the front desk and Alex headed up. Mendy was already there, waiting outside the room for his client.

"Anything I should know before we go in?"

"Alex, let me do as much of the talking as possible. Don't say a word directly to them without clearing it with me first."

He opened the door and the two men walked in to see a space with a desk and several chairs, but none of the usual hotel furniture. This was an interview room and nothing more. Alex spotted a refrigerator in the corner and noticed the smell of freshly brewed coffee. Dewey and Jervis McCracken sat at the table, and they both rose when Alex and Mendy arrived.

Two seats had been arranged on the other side of the table to the cops, and Dewey's hand indicated for them to sit down.

"I am glad you came today."

Alex glanced at Mendy, but said nothing as he had been instructed.

"My client is coming here of his own free will to assist the police in any way that he can."

"Well, counselor. Let's hope what you say is true."

Jervis took out a notebook and started scribbling, much to Alex's annoyance.

"You have been evading your fiscal duties from the day you arrived in this country, Mr. Cohen. That is a federal crime and, worse than that, your business dealings have been entirely illegal. I intend to prosecute you to the full extent of the law, do y'hear?"

"My client has conducted himself in an exemplary manner all his life—he's a war hero for goodness' sake—and has never been arrested or even charged with any crime."

"Notwithstanding his record, Mr. Cohen has been leading a crooked life and now he must pay the price."

"What are you offering?"

"If he gives us details of his criminal dealings, then he will walk free—no prison term and no fine."

"You want me to spill my guts about my friends?" Alex burst out. Mendy placed a hand gently on his client's arm and leaned towards Alex's ear. "He wants to make you respond. Don't give him the satisfaction. Let me speak for you."

Then he sat back, patted Alex's arm, and took over.

"As you can see, my client finds the consequences of what you are offering unpalatable. What else do you have for us?"

"We can still get him for racketeering."

"Mr. Dewey, you mistake me for an imbecile. You know as well as I do that to make a racketeering charge stick, you will need considerably more than a bunch of invoices and income statements. And if you had that kind of evidence, then we would meet downtown and not in some hovel like this. So let's be realistic, shall we? A wise man knows his reach."

Dewey's cheeks reddened and his partner continued to scratch away at his notepad.

"Your client has stolen money from the US Government and he must be punished for that crime. I demand justice for the American people."

"You want a big name to drag into the mud and anything else is a cherry on the top."

"Three million in back tax and a year in jail."

"My client has no desire to mix with criminals—he fought in the Great War—and the amount of damages you seek is punitive. Mr. Cohen isn't made of gelt."

Alex leaned over to Mendy. "Is this it? I lose most of my money?"

"Dewey wants your head on a spike so I can try to get you to pay less but you must hand something over otherwise there is no deal. Besides, if you don't pay a significant sum then Dewey won't be satisfied and will investigate you more—you and your business partners. And that is not advisable."

"Mendy, to do that means I must admit I am guilty, but all I have done is work hard all my life."

"Are you telling me you don't want me to cut you a deal?"

A thousand thoughts zoomed through Alex's mind. He wanted rid of Dewey, but his pride wouldn't let him be convicted of this crime. He couldn't rat out his friends, and that was the only way to free himself from Dewey's grasp now and in the future.

"No deal, Mendy. The *farbissener momzer* can *zoygn meyn hon*."

June 1936

35

THERE WAS SOMETHING Alex needed to resolve before he faced Dewey in court. He traveled out to his Hoboken apartment before placing a call with Sarah. He'd told Mendy of his plans because the last thing he wanted was to be stopped by the cops because he was crossing the state line when he was trying to see his family again.

The boys responded in their predictable manner, which Alex had accepted was normal several years ago. No matter what he thought, children were honest in their behavior—always—and he could pretend to himself that his absence made no difference to them and he could turn up whenever he wanted, but it was not true.

Instead, they visited him in the apartment and the oldest two did their best to ignore the fact that he existed. Massimo and Ezra were kind enough to join him and to help with the kids, but they had grown accustomed to the tykes so it wasn't that bad a day for these hardened killers.

At Alex's suggestion, Sarah arrived early to pick up the kids and he used the time to speak with her while the children were in the park.

"Thank you for letting me see the boys at such short notice, Sarah. I know my appearing in their lives is inconvenient at best. I have not been a good father to them and not an adequate husband to you."

Sarah walked to the other side of the living room and stared out of the window, arms crossed. Alex had hoped for a different reaction— silence was not how she was supposed to respond.

"I might be able to do something about becoming a better father, although we both know that is unlikely. But I sure can do something about being a better husband."

Sarah spun round, anger in her eyes.

"If you think I will take you back…"

"That's the last thing in the world I was thinking. Sarah, we can't relive our past, but I can offer you a better future. You deserve a divorce from me and that is what I want to give you."

A tear fell from her left eye, which she rubbed off with the back of her palm, and then she ran toward Alex and gave him a hug.

"Thank you, Alex Cohen."

A fire in Alex's stomach ignited as soon as he felt her touch, so he held on to the embrace far longer than he should have, although Sarah did not try to pull away either. It was almost like they both realized this was the last moment they would have together—their final time as a couple, even though they'd stopped living with each other years before. This moment in the Hoboken apartment room was the end of their relationship and, whether they recognized it or not, they both hurt.

She kissed him on the cheek and they separated. To extinguish the fluttering in his belly, Alex offered a coffee which Sarah gladly accepted. They wandered into the kitchen and he made their drinks.

"I'm not sure whether it's hit the New Jersey papers yet, but I will be on trial soon—for tax evasion."

"What are your chances?"

"Not great, according to my lawyer, and he should know."

"Is that why you're agreeing to the divorce?"

"I might be gone some time and you probably don't want the boys to be Cohens while I am away. I understand entirely."

"That's sweet of you."

"And as I have an attorney on retainer—I got Mendy to put together the paperwork for us."

Alex took a glug of his drink and sped into the hallway where he'd left his case. He opened it, removed a brown envelope, and returned to the kitchen table.

"This is for you, Sarah."

She squinted at the package, trying to imagine what it contained and then ripped it open to find the divorce papers inside.

"It's only fair that we get this sorted now. I don't want to have it hanging over me when I'm facing Dewey in court."

He pulled out a pen and placed it on the table.

"Shouldn't I hire a lawyer to check these over?"

"Of course, but it's a fair settlement. You get a million and there's another million in total held in trust for our sons. Sign today and I'll move the cash on Monday—then we hop over to Reno to make it legit."

Sarah picked up the documents and started to read the legal prose.

"I have always been straight with you, Sarah, with money. I only ever lied to you about where I was and who I was with."

She glanced up and carried on reading. Two seconds later, she stopped, put the papers down and picked up the pen.

"Where do I sign?"

Alex rifled through the sheets and showed her where to place her signature. Sarah's hand shook throughout the whole process, but she wrote her name in all the correct places. She placed the pen on the table and Alex picked it up and signed himself.

"I'll ask Ezra and Massimo to be our witnesses. Mendy will file everything the same day you get the money."

"You understand it was never about money."

"Gelt is only important if you don't have any. As soon as you do, there's always more significant things to worry about."

Sarah squeezed his hand and another tear dribbled out of her eye. Then a second and a third until she was crying full pelt. Alex collected her in his arms and did his best to soothe her pain.

"You are a free woman now. I hope you find happiness—and that you'll let me still be a part of your life somehow."

"There's the boys. I never want you to stop being with your sons."

"If I'm not in jail, I'll do my very best."

"I love you, Alex Cohen."

"And I love you too, Sarah Fleischman."

36

"DEWEY DUG UP a bunch of whores to testify against me. The jury believed that I collected envelopes from the madams myself. Then they were told I ran the biggest prostitution ring in New York. How does that add up, Alex?"

"He nailed you over tax, Charlie. Your paper income and your lifestyle didn't tally. That's what did for you."

The two men were sat in a cubicle at the heart of Sing Sing—Charlie's power and wealth had secured him a more pleasant jail experience than an ordinary Joe. He had dismissed the prison guard who had entered the room to accompany them during their conversation.

"Alex, if you are visiting just to harangue this panderer then leave me now."

"Not at all—forgive me. I have been spending a lot of time recently trying to understand how Dewey thinks and figure out what happens in tax evasion trials."

Charlie laughed out loud and raised a hand to show there was no disrespect.

"Sorry, Alex. I ignored Dewey until it was all too late. I see that you are doing your best not to make the same mistake."

"My day in court is around the corner."

"It always boils down to taxation in this country. They talk about streets paved with gold, but Uncle Sam wants you to pay for the privilege."

"We should have taken notice of what happened to Alfonse—he was on top of the world and was brought to his knees by not listening to his accountant. You know how he's doing?"

"Not really. Last I heard he was keeping his head down and doing his time like a model prisoner."

"How the mighty fall, Alex."

"That's not you, Charlie. Capone kept a high profile, and they clipped his wings when he flew too close to the sun. You are not him."

"Damn straight."

"So how can I help you keep running the syndicate?"

Charlie leaned in like the conspirator he was, and Alex mimicked the move.

"As much as I would want you to be my contact, that cannot be allowed to happen—not just because of your present difficulties, but because you need some plausible deniability and visiting me once a month is too dangerous for you if you do get off the current rap."

"I understand. What would you want me to do in the meantime, Charlie?"

"Contact my lieutenant, Vito Genovese. He will be responsible for day-to-day operations until I leave this place."

"The judge gave you a minimum of thirty years—you digging a tunnel?"

"Not me: Mendy. We have several lines of appeal he's working on. If everything goes to plan then I'll be out before Christmas and we can all celebrate New Year at the Waldorf Astoria Ball."

Alex wasn't convinced by Charlie's optimism. If Mendy was as direct with his friend as he was with Alex, the chances were that Luciano was not dealing with the information he was being told. Anyway, the fella was in jail and needed some hope on the horizon otherwise he'd die trapped inside these four walls. His sentence was ridiculously long—Dewey really had a point to prove, and the judge had helped him all the way.

While he wanted to be the kingpin in Charlie's plan, he understood that Genovese was the better choice—the man had been with Charlie since the start of Prohibition, could be trusted to the end of the world and wasn't about to stand trial for tax evasion.

"Is there anything else you'd like me to do for you?"

"Alex, it is kind of you to offer, but you need to focus on your own problems. Whatever you do, listen to Mendy's advice—he's a standup guy and knows what he's doing. If he gets you off, then sure you can help me some more and hopefully we'll be back at Lindy's in a few months having coffee and cheesecake. And if they put you behind bars or I don't get out on appeal, then none of this matters because we won't see each other again."

Charlie Luciano stared at Alex, inhaled, and let out a deep sigh. This was one hell of a way to say goodbye and that was how it felt like to Alex. They shook hands and hugged briefly. Then Charlie patted him on the shoulder. They separated and Alex walked out of Sing Sing, not knowing if he would ever see his friend again.

SEPTEMBER 1936

37

ALBERT HAD CALLED for a meeting of the heads of Murder Corporation, which was unusual as they normally only got together to assign contracts and not much else. Alex agreed as he wanted to gain a better idea of what was going on inside the man's head. Also, at the back of his mind was the notion he should confront both Anastasia and Buchalter over their assault on his heroin business.

The chosen location was Louis' Brownsville office and while he would have usually preferred to remain Midtown, secretly Alex was pleased to leave his old stomping ground for a few hours. When he arrived, there was something afoot—not one person was on the sidewalk and no other car was on the street. The entire block was deserted apart from a lone foot soldier standing in front of the building.

"What gives?"

"Park around the corner, please, Alex. We just want to make sure that you fellas can have a private meeting."

While that explanation made little sense, Alex did as he was asked and entered the joint from the service access at the rear. Although he had been doing this since he joined the syndicate, the irony was lost on Alex that men as powerful as he was used the same entrance as the janitor.

Stood outside the doorway was another of Anastasia's guys who frisked him before he could make his way inside. This had never happened before.

"What's with the extra security? You expecting trouble?"

"I just figured we should all be certain that everybody is safe here, that's all, Alex."

"Albert, you've brought your people here to keep Louis' building secure? What are you playing at?"

"This is no game, Alex. We have some serious matters to discuss. Let's not worry about the hired hands."

Alex shrugged and sat down opposite Anastasia and Buchalter, who offered him a coffee before proceedings began.

"There are two items on the agenda. The first is your court case, Alex."

"Dewey wants to take me down for tax evasion. My attorney says I have an excellent chance of beating the rap, so what is there to discuss?"

"I admire your optimism, Alex, and the fact that you still retain Mendy Greenberg as your attorney after what he did with Charlie."

"He's a good lawyer—the best money can buy."

"He is a shiny suit and a smile who has a certificate in a frame on his wall. Don't be fooled by his smooth talking and arrogant swagger —he's just another tinpot hack, soaking up the fees. When the government has taken all your money, you won't see him for dust."

"Thanks for the legal advice, Albert. I'll bear that in mind."

Louis broke the ensuing silence by regaling his companions with a tale of how he shot a lawyer in the *tuches* for a reason that Alex didn't care to listen to because he was wondering why Anastasia felt the need to undermine his choice of Mendy.

By the time the story had fizzled out with no one laughing at the punchline, Alex had mentally returned to the room and Albert had taken back control of the conversation.

"Your situation means we must make some changes at Murder Corporation."

"Why is that, Albert?"

"With all due respect, you are about to spend several weeks if not months embroiled in a court case and throughout that time, you won't be able to fulfill your duties—nor would we expect you to. Beating the cops is more important, right, Louis?"

"Of course, Albert."

"So we think it best if you were to temporarily step down from running the operation until all this Dewey business is behind you. After, you can come back just as before. It's for your own good."

"Kind of you to be so concerned about my welfare, again."

Alex created a pause by sipping his coffee before continuing.

"And will I still receive my compensation while I am no longer on active duty?"

Anastasia glanced at Louis and turned his attention back to Alex.

"Why, of course. This isn't about money—it's giving you the best chance to get through this legal difficulty you face and for the rest of us to know there's nothing you do that will catch the eye of Dewey or any of the other cops."

"If you want to pay me for doing absolutely nothing, how could I refuse?"

"Good, that's settled."

The door opened and Abe Reles appeared, mumbled something, and headed to the kitchen area. The noise of the boiling kettle rumbled through the room, but everybody ignored it.

"Albert, you said there were two items for us to discuss. What was the second?"

"We need to mop up the Joe Rosen business. Alex, would you mind sorting this out because everyone has been patient. He might not have spilled anything to Dewey." A quick glance at Louis to acknowledge all his disquiet, who picked up the conversation. "But we still need to show that his behavior has been unacceptable."

"You want me to handle this matter before I step down, Louis?"

"Think of it as a last hurrah, Alex."

"You said this was only for a few months."

"You know what I meant, I'm sure."

"Yes, I'll organize the Rosen hit."

Reles walked through the room and out the door.

◆ ◆ ◆

"MEYER, THEY'VE TAKEN Murder Corporation away from me, and Albert has stolen Charlie's narcotics trafficking and nobody is doing anything to stop them."

"There's concern about you, Alex."

"Who?"

"They think you might cut a deal with Dewey to save yourself from jail."

"What do you reckon, Meyer?"

"I trust you, Alex. You know I do, I hope."

"Why isn't anyone else showing me the same courtesy?"

"It's not like that, Alex. Not everyone knows you as well as Charlie, Benny and me. The rest of them see a man who has been cornered by Dewey, and Charlie is looking at thirty to fifty years in jail. Are you prepared for that stretch? The only thing holding Charlie together is the belief that Mendy will get him out on appeal."

"I'm not in the same league as Charlie."

"It doesn't matter if it is true—people act on what they believe, Alex."

"And they expect me to squeal."

"Many of us would be tempted. Nobody wants to spend the rest of their lives in jail—even doing gangster time. The bars still won't go away."

"Just between you and me, Meyer, I considered it—of course I did. But I've chosen to face Dewey in court. I can't bring myself to plead guilty and take a plea because the prosecutor will have me under his thumb from now until the day I die. So I'm going to fight Dewey and convince the jury and the judge not to convict."

"Pleased to hear that, Alex. For some, that is enough, but for the likes of Anastasia, your pleading not guilty merely counts as a good start."

"So the only way Anastasia will trust me again is if I go to jail?"

"Pretty much. The longer the sentence, the more you'll be safe in their eyes."

"Do you know how crazy that sounds?"

"We live in a strange world, Alex. What can I tell you?"

Alex glanced round Meyer's suite and thought back on all the conversations which had taken place here with his friends—the hours spent with Arnold Rothstein, Charlie and the rest. And he wondered if he would see the Benjamin Hotel interior again.

38

ALEX KEPT THE Rosen hit nice and simple, so he asked Ezra if he'd like to take a ride and make some money along the way. The trip to Brooklyn took no time at all and soon they had parked in a dark corner of town and were agreeing how to handle the situation.

"The hardest part will be to find him and then wait until he is alone. This must not become a bloodbath. In, shoot, out. Got it, Ezra?"

"Sure thing. You have much on him?"

"He used to drive a truck and now he doesn't. We can't be sure, but he probably isn't packing a gun. That's all I got."

Ezra nodded at the acknowledgment of their collective ignorance.

"We'd better take a walk and see who we find, boss."

They hopped out of the black saloon, pushed their hats down over their eyes and turned up their collars. Then they headed to the corner of Brooklyn that Rosen called home—his candy store in Brownsville.

The frontage was nothing much to look at—Rosen Candy Store written in large letters on a sign running the front of the place, a window filled with trays of confection and a glass door. Everything was open to the light, hoping to entice passers-by to pop in and make a purchase. Alex and Ezra hung back across the street fifty feet along so that Rosen wouldn't notice two men staring at his store and not coming in.

"He spends almost all his time alone, which is great, but if anyone walks past, they will see us while we are in there."

"I agree, Ezra. Why don't we wait to see where he goes after he shuts up the joint this afternoon?"

FOR THE NEXT three hours, they took it in turns to skulk around in the shadows near the store. This gave the other an opportunity to grab a bite to eat and hide in their vehicle.

Alex watched the joint and glanced at his watch for the hundredth time that afternoon. For a fella whose only life skill was to drive from one city to another, Rosen had a surprisingly thriving little candy store—not exactly rammed with customers lining up and down the street, but a handful of people an hour to keep the wolf from the door. Alex guessed that the guy made most of his money after school and at weekends. His watch told him there would be a surge of youthful activity in the next ten minutes—and he wasn't wrong.

By six, Rosen seemed to pack up and eventually the lights went out. The trucker appeared at the door, locked up and headed down the sidewalk. Ezra had just arrived a minute before, so they agreed to split up and tail the candy guy hoping to find an opportunity that evening. Rosen walked one street south and then another east until he reached an apartment block and entered.

"He'll be in the bosom of his family now, Alex."

"Yep. Let's stick around for a short while in case he has to pop out for something, otherwise we're stuck until morning."

They smoked and waited fifteen long minutes, but nobody appeared.

"We could enter his apartment and take him out."

"Ezra, we really don't want any witnesses. That is the last thing I need—to be implicated in a homicide just before my tax evasion trial. It's bad enough that Anastasia has put me on this job without you getting us both tried for murder."

"I was merely trying to run through the options we got if we want to do for him this evening like you said you wanted. I thought I was helping."

"Sorry, Ezra, but in future only voice ideas you think will work out. I keep my dumbass thoughts to myself."

Another ten minutes and they had both spent more than enough time for one day in Brownsville.

"I have an idea, Ezra. Pick me up at five. Don't look at me like that —I know it's early. If everything works the way I hope then I'll buy you a slap-up breakfast at Lindy's."

EZRA HALTED HIS stolen vehicle around the rear of Rosen's candy store. The car was different from yesterday's and had been in an underground parking lot controlled by Ezra at least four weeks and had only seen the light of day when Ezra drove it to Alex's place and out to Brownsville. Needless to say, the plates had been boosted from another car a week before.

At eight, they heard a rustling inside the store and a minute later, Rosen opened the back door and stood by the entrance to enjoy a cigarette. Having drained the last vestige of tobacco from his smoke, Rosen threw the butt on the ground and returned to his work indoors.

"Shall we take him now?"

"Ezra, let's wait a short while. I figure a guy like Rosen is used to hard work but would still prefer to stay in bed than open up this early. My guess is that there will be a delivery soon and we don't want to get caught by an eyewitness."

Alex's patience bore fruit as five minutes after their conversation, a delivery truck drew up and Rosen signed for two enormous boxes of candies, taking them inside. When the vehicle had gone around the corner and vanished from sight, Alex nudged Ezra and both men got out of the saloon and edged toward the rear entrance of the place.

They waited fifteen seconds and Alex popped his head inside the joint, opened the door fully, and Ezra followed him in. They reached the front of the store and found Rosen behind the counter, bent down, unpacking his merchandise with the shades pulled down in the front door and windows. Their footsteps must have been louder than intended because he stood up and turned round.

"What can I do for you guys? You know we're not open yet."

Alex shrugged, looked at Ezra who copied his boss, then both men pulled out their revolvers and shot the former trucker in the chest, two slugs each. Alex stepped forward, careful not to walk in the ever-growing pool of blood to check the guy was dead.

"Let's get out of here. Once we've dumped the pieces and the car, we can take a cab in Manhattan over to Lindy's. I owe you a mighty breakfast."

39

THE DAY BEFORE the start of his trial, Alex paid a nafka to spend the evening with him. He informed her he would call her Rebecca, as he did on the rare occasion he hired female companionship. To make sure he gave himself a good night's sleep, he consumed most of a bottle of Scotch—Rebecca preferred a cosmo but Alex wasn't focused on keeping her happy.

After they ate steak and fries in his suite, he took her to bed but the only intimacy between them was that he curled round her and the two naked people fell asleep. The following morning, he slapped her ass to wake her and encouraged her to leave so he could have breakfast alone. Then downstairs and out to the waiting car wearing his finest suit.

The camera flashes popped in his face when he arrived at the courthouse; the press asking questions he had no intention of answering. Alex did his best to hide behind his fedora as he didn't want to be seen on the front page of the late editions. When he found the courtroom, Mendy smiled as he walked towards the lawyer.

"Let's go to a meeting room so we can have a private conversation."

Alex nodded and followed Mendy out of the court, filled with oak and the musty aroma of piles of paper, and headed over the corridor about twenty feet to the left.

"To work, then, Alex. All I want you to do is to keep your hands visible on the table, don't scowl at anything you hear or at anything that Dewey does. Finally, every so often glance at the jury. If you never make eye contact with them, you'll behave like a guilty man and that is not the impression we are trying to convey, right?"

"I am only guilty of being an industrious American."

"Save it for the jury."

A WEEK LATER and Alex had done his best to follow Mendy's instructions and at least held back from delivering an outburst like the one that erupted out of his lips when he last met Dewey. In the meantime, the special prosecutor laid out the lavish apartments, hotel suites and other real estate under Alex's control. By the time the court had waded through all that detail, it was Friday afternoon.

Then he worked his way through Alex's tax affairs, such as they were. Thirty minutes later and there was nothing more to say and the case for the prosecution rested, so the judge called for a recess until Monday. Before they left for the night, Mendy and Alex scooted back to their room down the corridor to take stock.

"What do you think, Mendy?"

"The evidence has piled high and it felt like Dewey found anyone who has seen you spend a dime and put them on the stand."

"We knew this would happen—you warned me the first day we met."

"Yes Alex, but I've been keeping my eye on the jury and the way they look at you. I can assure you this isn't going well. Most of them don't bother turning to see your reaction to the evidence anymore. That is not a good sign."

"So how do we counter Dewey?"

"Would you like me to see if he'll cut you a deal?"

"No. If I do that then no syndicate member'll trust me again. They will always assume that I spilled my guts to Dewey—which is what he wants me to do anyway, right?"

"Alex, if we fight to the bitter end, I cannot guarantee you won't do hard time."

"I'd rather accept that risk then wind up stabbed on the street on my way home one night—or worse."

"Dewey has taken the jury's heads. Why don't we try to grab at their hearts? Would you be prepared to take the stand, Alex?"

"Whatever you think will work."

"We can present you as an upright fella with a wife and family— and some commercial interests on the side."

"I signed the divorce papers last week."

"Until a trip to Reno they are just bits of paper. You, on the other hand, are a family guy who runs a small business—work with me here."

ON MONDAY, FIRST thing, Alex was sworn in and took the stand. Mendy got Alex to describe his domestic situation.

"Mr. Cohen. Where do you live?"

"In a hotel suite in midtown."

"And is that your only residence?"

"No, sir. I also have a small place in Hoboken."

"Why do you need a second home? Most New Yorkers aren't lucky enough to have two."

"My wife and children are there and I try to spend as much time with them as I possibly can. I work late in the city so I have somewhere to sleep here too."

"So you don't acquire real estate like toys in a box?"

"No, I am just a guy trying to get by."

"Thank you, Mr. Cohen. I'm sure your sons appreciate your care. What age are they?"

"Objection!"

"Sustained. Keep your questions relevant, Mr. Greenberg."

"Are your children old enough to visit you on their own in Manhattan?"

"No, I must go to them. They are aged between nine and fourteen years."

"Alex, the prosecution's contention is that you are a criminal who has never paid his taxes. Have you filed tax returns?"

"Of course I have. I am a good American, but I am no accountant. When I came to this country I was only fifteen and couldn't even speak the language. I didn't have a trade, but I learned fast and have earned enough to take care of my family. If my tax filings have been a few cents out, then I ask that the jury forgives me. I was more worried about feeding my kin than recording items in a ledger."

"Thank you. No further questions."

Mendy took a while to sit down and gave Alex time to relax before Dewey's cross-examination. He eyeballed as many jurors as he could. Perhaps if they saw Alex as a human and not as a bunch of papers and numbers then he might have a chance. The wily prosecutor raised off his haunches and pounded straight to the witness box, standing inches away from Alex's face.

"How many residences do you own, Mr. Cohen?"

"Two."

"That's not true. The court has already seen that your name is on the deeds of four properties. You know the evidence put before the jury, same as them."

"But…"

"And what is your business?"

"I import a variety of goods."

"What kind?"

"Food, drink, that sort of thing in the main."

"And have you ever been paid to carry out any criminal activity?"

"Of course, not. I am a respectable American."

"So you keep saying, Cohen."

"You have made many claims about me, Mr. Dewey. Just because you say something does not make it so. A good American looks after his family, helps his friends, and supports his country. I went to fight in Europe and survived while you were still playing ball in high school."

"This trial isn't about your war record. This is about whether you have paid your taxes. Did you file them last year?"

"Yes."

"But where are the documents? There are no records to support what you say."

"I know I filed them and I supplied you with a copy many months ago."

The eyes of the jury switched from Alex to Dewey—the first chink in Dewey's armor despite an onslaught that had lasted a week.

MENDY AND ALEX sat with a coffee in their private room that lunchtime, knowing that closing arguments would commence in the afternoon.

"Did we do well this morning, Mendy?"

"You scored a few points against Dewey but I don't know if it has been enough. I still recommend you let me speak to him right now and get a deal lined up."

"I've told you before and I will say it again: no. That cannot happen."

While they waited, Alex and Mendy remained in their room, drinking and eating. Mendy had ordered a takeout from Lindy's so at least Alex could enjoy a piece of cheesecake.

Then an officer of the court knocked politely and told them the jury had reached a verdict, so they trundled back into the courtroom. As Alex rose to hear the pronouncement, the foreman announced that yes, they had reached a verdict upon which they all agreed.

"How say you in this matter?"

"We find the defendant guilty."

Alex didn't hear another word anyone in court spoke that afternoon. Everything became a blur in his head.

A month later when they came back to the courthouse for sentencing, Mendy told him that five years was not as bad as it could have been and Dewey grinned before leaving the court to pontificate to the press outside.

Ida was dead; after a trip to Nevada, Sarah was no longer his wife. Meyer, Benny, and the rest of the syndicate had turned their backs on him. Anastasia and Louis had stolen the heroin trafficking racket from under him and no one had done anything to stop them. Not even Charlie, who hadn't lifted a finger to intervene.

When those five long years were over, Alex wouldn't be able to stay on the East Coast because none of the syndicate would speak to him. Despite serving time, there would be the suspicion that he had given some of them up to Dewey. After all, why had he only received such a short sentence when Alfonse had received ten and Charlie was looking at spending the rest of his life in jail.

As he was led onto the waiting bus to take him to Rikers, Alex was alone—no wife, no mistress, no friends, no family. Not even the promise that his business partners would look after him while he was behind bars or when he came out. All that remained was the memory of the scent of a woman he called Rebecca and the lingering taste of cheesecake under his breath.

THE END

THANK YOU FOR READING!

Get a free novella

Building a relationship with my readers is the very best thing about writing. I send weekly newsletters with details of new releases, special offers and other bits of news relating to my novels.

And if you sign up to the mailing list I'll send you a copy of the Lagotti Family prequel, The Stickup. Just go to www.leob.ws/signup and we'll take it from there.

Enjoy this book? You can make a difference

Reviews are the most powerful tools in my arsenal when it comes to getting attention for my books. Much as I'd like to, I don't have the financial muscle of a New York publisher. I can't take out full page ads or put posters on the subway. (Not yet, anyway).

But I do have something much more powerful and effective than that, and it's something that those publishers would kill to get their hands on.

A committed and loyal bunch of readers.

Honest reviews of my books help bring them to the attention of other readers.

If you've enjoyed this book I shall be very grateful if you would spend just five minutes leaving a review (it can be as short as you like) on the book's page. You can jump right to the page by clicking www.books2read.com/huckster.

Thank you very much.

Leo

SNEAK PREVIEW

In Book 4, Casino Chiseler…

Bulbs popped and whizzed round his head as the crime reporters swarmed around him, hoping to catch the best photo of Alex for their front page noon editions. Local cops lined his route from the kerbside to the court entrance. Perhaps for the first time in his life, he was grateful to a bunch of flatfeet.

The crowd thickened at the bottom of the courthouse steps, forcing Mendy and Alex to pause their attempts to proceed.

"What you going to tell Kefauver?"

"Are you naming any names today?"

"How does it feel to be back in court?"

A thousand questions whirred around his ears as each reporter did their best to get their quote for their editor, but Alex followed Mendy's instructions and said nothing.

Although a handful of reporters stayed with them as they entered the hallowed portals of the courthouse building and Mendy asked a nearby court official where they needed to go. The answer delivered them to a wide corridor packed with men and women standing around, looking like they had as much idea what was going on as Alex did.

"Brace yourself, the world and his wife is watching us."

Into the courtroom and an usher took them to the front right-hand benches. Alex surveyed the joint: an arc of seats for the senators to question their witnesses, sat opposite with a bank of tables and chairs for them and their lawyers. Behind them, the auditorium packed with a mixture of concerned citizens, members of the press and court ghouls who'd turn up to the opening of a paper bag if it took place in this building.

To the wings, either side of the tables in front of the politicians' pews were enormous boxes on wheels—the TV cameras. Alex swallowed hard. Mendy nudged him and leaned in.

"Don't worry about the television crew. They are not your enemy —the senators are the ones who'll question you. Everything else is fluff. Stick to the script and if you think you will deviate from the plan, then stop and speak with me."

A hush entered the room and Alex twisted round to see what was happening. If he had bothered to remain facing forwards, he would have seen a side door open and a stream of men gush into the courtroom and take their seats in the arc in front of him. No sooner had they appeared than the lights on the top of the television cameras glowed red, showing they were live on air across the country.

After an interminable wait for everyone to sit down, open their cases, shuffle their papers and settle into their seats, the first witness was called. Alex stood up and sat down in the center of the tables with Mendy by his side.

A court official stepped toward him and asked Alex to swear to tell the truth, the whole truth and pretty much only the truth before his God. When this activity started, the TV cameras swung round and focused their rays on him. Despite being unsettled by this mechanical response, Alex sat down, leaning forward so that his elbows rested on the table and he interleaved the fingers of one hand in between those on the other. Then he exhaled and stared forwards and the cockroach immediately in front of Estes Kefauver.

"Let's keep this simple shall we, gentlemen?"

Those beady eyes bore inside him and Alex swallowed hard again.

"Mr. Cohen, let me remind you that you are under oath. Are you, or have you ever been, an active participant in the organized crime syndicate known as the mafia?"

"No, I have never been a member of the mafia."

To grab your copy, go to www.leob.ws/chiseler.

OTHER BOOKS BY THE AUTHOR

Alex Cohen

The Bowery Slugger (Book 1)
East Side Hustler (Book 2)
Midtown Huckster (Book 3)
Alex Cohen Books 1-3 (Due Late 2020)
Casino Chiseler (Book 4–Due Late 2020)
Cuban Heel (Book 5–Due 2021)
Hollywood Bilker (Book 6–Due 2021)
The Mensch (Book 7–Due 2021)
Alex Cohen Books 4-7 (Due 2022)

Stand Alone

The Case
The Death and Life of Penny Pitstop (erotic)
Awakenings (erotic, serialized)

The Lagotti Family

The Heist (Book 1)
The Getaway (Book 2)
Powder (Book 3)
Mama's Gone (Book 4)
The Lagotti Family Complete Collection (Books 1-4)

All books are available from www.leob.ws and all major eBook and paperback sales platforms.

ABOUT THE AUTHOR

Leopold Borstinski is an independent author whose past careers have included financial journalism, business management of financial software companies, consulting and product sales and marketing, as well as teaching.

There is nothing he likes better so he does as much nothing as he possibly can. He has travelled extensively in Europe and the US and has visited Asia on several occasions. Leopold holds a Philosophy degree and tries not to drop it too often.

He lives near London and is married with one wife, one child and no pets.

Find out more at LeopoldBorstinski.com.